"Are You Afraid Of Me?"
Jase Asked.

"Not at all," Leslie replied.

"I would never take advantage of you," he said softly. "Please believe me."

She turned and looked at his shadowy figure. "I do."

"Leslie?" There was a long pause. "Never mind."

She walked over to him and knelt beside his bed. "Tell me, Jason."

He sighed. "I was thinking we could stay warmer if we shared a bed. I told you it was stupid. Good night," he said abruptly.

"Jason? Do you want me to sleep with you?"

Dear Reader,

Sit back, relax and indulge yourself with all the fabulous offerings from Silhouette Desire this October. Roxanne St. Claire is penning the latest DYNASTIES: THE ASHTONS with *The Highest Bidder*. Youngest Ashton sibling, Paige, finds herself participating in a bachelorette auction and being "won" by a sexy stranger. Strangers also make great protectors, as demonstrated by Annette Broadrick in *Danger Becomes You*, her most recent CRENSHAWS OF TEXAS title.

Speaking of protectors, Michelle Celmer's heroine in *Round-the-Clock Temptation* gets a bodyguard of her very own: a member of the TEXAS CATTLEMAN'S CLUB. Linda Conrad wraps up her miniseries THE GYPSY INHERITANCE with *A Scandalous Melody*. Will this mysterious music box bring together two lonely hearts? For something a little darker, why not try *Secret Nights at Nine Oaks* by Amy J. Fetzer? A handsome recluse, an antebellum mansion—two great reasons to stay indoors. And be sure to catch Heidi Betts's *When the Lights Go Down*, the story of a plain-Jane librarian out to make some serious changes in her humdrum love life.

As you can see, Silhouette Desire has lots of great stories for you to enjoy. So spend this first month of autumn cuddled up with a good book—and come back next month for even more fabulous reads.

Enjoy!

Melissa Jeglinski

Melissa Jeglinski
Senior Editor
Silhouette Desire

Please address questions and book requests to:
Silhouette Reader Service
U.S.: 3010 Walden Ave., P.O. Box 1325, Buffalo, NY 14269
Canadian: P.O. Box 609, Fort Erie, Ont. L2A 5X3

ANNETTE BROADRICK

DANGER BECOMES YOU

Published by Silhouette Books

America's Publisher of Contemporary Romance

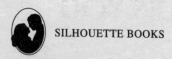 SILHOUETTE BOOKS

ISBN 0-373-76682-3

DANGER BECOMES YOU

Visit Silhouette Books at www.eHarlequin.com

Printed in U.S.A.

ANNETTE BROADRICK

believes in romance and the magic of life. Since 1984, Annette has shared her view of life and love with readers. In addition to being nominated by *Romantic Times* magazine as one of the Best New Authors of that year, she has also won the *Romantic Times* Reviewers' Choice Award for Best in its Series; the *Romantic Times* WISH Award; and the *Romantic Times* magazine Lifetime Achievement Awards for Series Romance and Series Romantic Fantasy.

One

A slight sound outside the cabin brought Jason Crenshaw awake and on full alert. He must have fallen asleep while reading. Someone was outside despite the ferocity of the winter snowstorm that would keep any sensible person inside.

Could it be someone looking for him? He couldn't imagine who it could be. Only his commanding officer knew that he was using a friend's hunting cabin in Michigan to recuperate from his wounds.

Jase eased his way out of the chair and picked up his cane. He palmed his military-issue pistol out of habit and silently moved to the window.

He couldn't see the small porch and its overhang from this angle but he had a clear view of the driveway that led to the road. There were no tracks. Although the snow was blowing heavily, there was no way it could have covered tracks that quickly.

His years in Delta Force made him wary and alert to everything around him and he instinctively knew that what he'd heard, despite the loud fury of the storm, was someone stepping onto the single wooden step to the porch. Who was it and how did they get here?

He didn't like surprises and he especially didn't like unexpected guests.

A firm knock sounded and he edged to the locked door.

"Who's there?" he demanded. His voice sounded rusty from disuse.

"I'm sorry to bother you," a woman's shaking voice replied. "My car slid off the road and I'm stuck in a ditch. May I use your phone to call for help?"

He didn't like her story. The road that passed his house wasn't one of the main highways in the state. In fact, it ended at the lake about fifteen miles from here. What was she doing on this secondary road in the first place?

When he didn't answer, she spoke again. "Hello? I know I'm a bother, I just—"

He unlocked the door and opened it just enough to see the snow-encrusted figure in front of him. She wore a lightweight coat with a hood. The coat stopped at her thighs, revealing jeans and winter boots. Her eyes were the golden color of aged whiskey and her face looked pale as death.

The word he muttered was unprintable. Just what he needed: a damsel in distress when he wasn't in any shape or mood to play a blasted gallant knight.

He swung the door wide, the pistol at his side. "Get in so I can close the door."

She hurriedly stepped inside. After he slammed the door shut and locked it, he turned and caught the woman looking at him in abject terror, her gaze frozen on the pistol in his hand. What did she think he was going to do, shoot anyone who showed up at his door?

Without commenting on her obvious fear, he moved to the table and laid the pistol down.

He turned and stared at her still huddled by the door. She looked frozen.

Not his problem.

She was shaking.

Not his problem.

The snow she'd brought in was melting off her clothes and dripping onto the floor.

Now *that* was his problem.

"Look, lady. I have no intention of shooting you, so get that coat off before I have to wipe water off the floor."

"Oh!" She looked down and saw the puddle around her feet. She quickly slipped off her coat and looked around for a place to put it.

The electricity had gone off a couple of hours ago and the large rectangular room was in shadows except for the kerosene lantern on the table by the chair in which he'd been reading.

"There's a coatrack by the door," he said gruffly.

He watched her remove her gloves and hang up her coat before she wiped down her jeans with her hands. When she turned to look around the cabin, her face telegraphed her trepidation.

Jase knew what she saw. The cabin was one room that ended in an L-shaped alcove where the kitchen was located. Besides the table and chairs, there was a couch that had seen better days, a recliner that once had been overstuffed but now looked weary and two sets of bunk beds at the other end of the room, placed in opposite corners.

A potbellied stove vented through the roof sat in the middle of the room, radiating the only heat he had. The only other amenity was a small bathroom off the kitchen. He kept the door closed to conserve heat.

When she removed her hat he saw that she had short, feathery blond curls sticking up in tufts around her face. She was tall, slender and looked like a teenager.

Her eyes bespoke an innocence that he found unusual since she had a soft, full mouth that begged to be kissed.

Not that her looks meant anything to him, regardless of the fact he'd not seen a woman since he left the hospital. He knew he was no fit companion for anyone, most especially an innocent teenage girl.

He watched her pick up an old towel hanging near the door and hastily clean up the puddle of water. He refused to do more than glance at the way her jeans cupped her butt and clung to her long, shapely legs when she bent over.

Jase looked away, irritated by his awareness of her. He set his cane aside, wincing at the protesting places where bullets had been removed from his shoulder, side and thigh, and sat in the captain's chair he'd been occupying before she arrived.

The pain brought him back to the present, reminding him why he had chosen to be alone through his recuperation. He'd retreated as far from his life as he could get. Not even his family knew where he was, which was exactly what he wanted.

When she straightened, he scowled at her. He didn't want her here, but even he wasn't cold-blooded enough to deny her some warmth and safety.

She attempted a smile that disappeared when he didn't respond. "If I could use your phone and call for road assistance, I'll be on my way." She twisted her fingers as though attempting to braid them.

He stared at her in silence. She had a soft drawl that spoke of the South, which might explain her clothing, which was unsuitable for a northern winter, and her clueless attitude about traveling during a storm.

"You may not have noticed that we're in the midst of a winter snowstorm. You aren't going to find anyone willing to risk life and limb to pull your car out of a snowbank until the storm passes."

She did her best to hide her panic, but he could see it in her eyes.

She turned away and reached for her coat.

"What are you doing now?" he demanded.

She looked over her shoulder. "I'll go back to my car until the storm passes."

He shook his head in disbelief. "Good thinking, Ms. Alabama," he drawled. "By all means, return to your car where you can freeze to death while waiting for the storm to blow over. It could last for days."

She turned slowly around to face him, her chin lifted. "My name is Leslie O'Brien and I'm from Tennessee, not Alabama. As for freezing, I'll do what I can to stay warm since that seems to be my only option at the moment."

Fine. Let her go. You don't want her here, so let her freeze.

Instead of voicing his thoughts Jase said, "Don't compound your foolishness with idiocy. You'll stay here until someone can get out here to help you." He nodded to his cane. "I'm afraid I can't help. I'm still learning to walk without falling."

Leslie folded her arms, her gaze glacial. "What, exactly, do you see as my foolishness?" she asked, ignoring his last remark.

"Being out in this kind of weather in the first place. Have you ever driven in snow before?"

Her mouth tightened. "As a matter of fact, I haven't. When I left the motel at dawn I didn't expect to run into a snowstorm. By the time the snowflakes began to fall, I was only thirty miles from my destination. I didn't expect the flakes to turn into a storm so quickly or that the road would be so slippery."

He shook his head wearily. "The fact remains that you're here for the duration. You might as well accept it."

His last comment was aimed at both of them.

He nodded to the coffeepot sitting on the woodstove. "As you can see, the electricity is out, which isn't unusual during a storm. There's coffee if you want some."

She nodded her head jerkily and walked over to the stove, holding her hands out for warmth. He grabbed his cane and went over to the galley-like kitchen to fetch another cup. As he returned to his captain's chair, he handed it to her.

She poured herself some coffee and, with something less than enthusiasm, approached the table, placing her cup at the opposite end from where he sat.

Instead of taking a seat she glanced around the room. "May I use your restroom?"

He nodded toward the door. "In there."

She hurried through the kitchen, opened the bathroom door and went inside, closing the door quietly behind her.

What in hell was he going to do with this woman? He couldn't send her back out into the storm to freeze to death. But he didn't want her here. The cabin hadn't been built for privacy. It served its purpose for the hunters who stayed for a few days at a time.

He was alone because that's the way he wanted it. He wanted to get back to normal before he faced the outside world. He needed a private place to wrestle with his demons.

Leslie leaned against the bathroom door and shivered. There was no heat in here. She wondered if the water was frozen. She hurriedly used the facilities and washed her hands with icy cold water. At least she was out of the wind.

What was she going to do?

She'd been running for three days, paying cash for gas, motels and food so she wouldn't be traced, but she felt far from safe. She'd counted on reaching the place her cousin owned, knowing she'd be safe because no one would think to look for her there. She needed a place to stay while she tried to figure out what to do next.

Her cousin Larry owned a two-story log cabin that his family used as a vacation spot. It was somewhere along this road, near the edge of one of the lakes in the region. She and her mother had visited with them for two weeks over several summers in years past, but everything had looked so different now, especially with the snow obscuring her vision.

She had no idea how close she was to his place. Before she'd slid into the ditch Leslie had begun to worry that she might miss the entrance to the long, private driveway that ended at the cabin.

The skies had been gray and a strong, cold wind had been blowing when she'd left the motel this morning. She'd had no idea that it was expected to snow.

The man in the other room was right: she hadn't understood what the signs meant or she might not have left the motel. However, once the snow began to fall she was only about thirty miles from Larry's place so she'd decided to keep going.

She'd panicked when the snowflakes quickly turned into thick sheets of white. She hadn't been able to see the road and had slowed to a crawl, peering through the windshield that the wiper blades couldn't clear fast enough.

Of course she wouldn't have deliberately driven out into a storm if she'd known one was coming. Regardless of what her curmudgeon host thought, she wasn't a complete fool.

Not that any of that mattered now. There was no way she could rewind her day to make a more informed decision, which placed her in an extremely awkward situation. She was faced with the very real possibility of freezing if she went back to her car. If she stayed, she would have to deal with the crabby stranger in the other room, which put her between a rock and a hard place.

Her luck was running out fast at a time when she desperately needed it. Of all the places where she might have gotten stuck, she'd managed to find one with a hermit who hated people. Or maybe he just hated women. Whatever it was, his total lack of enthusiasm in allowing her to stay had been obvious.

She couldn't tell how old he was. Possibly in his late thirties. He was tall with a lean build. She had no idea what was wrong with his leg. All she knew was that he didn't put much weight on it.

He appeared to have only a nodding acquaintance with a razor and a good haircut would go a long way to improve his appearance.

What she found most disconcerting about him were his eyes. They were almost a silvery blue that intensified his penetrating stare. They made clear that he'd sized her up and found her to be an inferior human being.

Leslie had been staring unseeing into the mirror until her reflection caught her eye. The dark circles under her eyes had circles. She looked like a raccoon. Outside of that, she was as pale as the snow outside.

She fished a comb out of her purse and ran it through her short hair. She'd cut it her first night on the run in an attempt to change her appearance. She'd never been the type of woman people noticed and she sincerely hoped she could pretend to be someone else if her situation grew dire.

Leslie shivered. She was going to get frostbite if she stayed in the bathroom for much longer. She stiffened her spine and opened the door, determined to be pleasant no matter how rude her reluctant host chose to be.

He hadn't moved from the chair he'd been in and seemed to be enthralled with the thick book in front of him.

She sat down and quietly sipped her coffee. She was glad she'd allowed it to cool a little. It was almost too hot to drink, even now. She waited for him to look up, to speak, to do something other than ignore her presence.

She finally gave up on that. "It would be helpful if I knew your name," she said, attempting to hide her irritation.

"Jason," he said without glancing at her.

Great. Jason with no last name. The pistol lay on the table beside his chair. Was he a criminal? Or maybe paranoid. Or a paranoid criminal.

She jumped when he raised his head and said, "If you're hungry, Miz Scarlett, there's a pot of stew in the

kitchen on the back burner of the stove. Help yourself."
He returned to his book, obviously feeling that his duties as a host were done.

As a matter of fact, she was starved; she hadn't stopped for more than gasoline since leaving the motel. She'd been eating junk food all day, which could be partially to blame for her shakes.

The rest was stark fear.

She walked into the kitchen area and lifted the lid of a large pot. The aroma almost made her groan with yearning. After opening two cabinet doors, she found an earthenware bowl and filled it with the savory stew.

"Would you like some?" she asked.

After a moment he replied, "Yeah. Thanks."

Now there was a grudging thanks if she'd ever heard one, but at least he'd put himself out to show a modicum of politeness. She filled another bowl and carried both of them to the table, placing his in front of him.

He closed the book and she handed him one of the spoons she'd stuck in her pocket. He immediately began to eat.

"When do you think the storm will be over?" she finally asked.

He took his time lifting his gaze to look at her. He shook his head and shrugged. "Sorry. No crystal ball." He went back to eating.

"Does the snow melt once it stops?"

He sighed. "Eventually. Probably by March."

"March! But that's two months from now!"

He looked at her without expression. "Somebody should have told you that winter in Michigan isn't the best place to vacation unless you enjoy winter sports."

Suddenly her appetite was gone.

At this rate, the snow would be piled so high she wouldn't be able to find the driveway to Larry's place after she got her car on the road again.

She sat listening to the sounds around her. She heard the pop and sizzle of wood in the stove, a tree branch brushing against the side of the cabin, the wind howling like a ghost in a horror movie. The smell of stew and coffee gave the cabin a pleasant aroma and the lamp on the table gave out a golden glow.

She studied the walls, where some kind of heavy caulking sealed any gaps between the large logs, and looked up at the slanted roof supported by thick lumber. Too bad the place didn't have a ceiling, as well, to trap the warm air that moved upward.

When Jason spoke, breaking the silence, she jumped in surprise.

"How did you find this place, anyway? I didn't see any tracks."

"I, uh, happened to see the smoke from your chimney while I was trying to figure a way to get the car out of the ditch. During a break in the wind I was looking to see a house or a light when I spotted the smoke. I began to walk in as straight a line as possible through the trees where there wasn't as much snow. I'll admit I was getting a little nervous until I finally spotted the cabin."

"Ah."

Leslie gathered their bowls after they'd finished eating and washed the dishes. She refilled their cups of coffee and, rather than sit at the table, wandered over to a nearby window to look out. Although her watch showed that the time was a little after three, light was fading fast.

If anything, the wind had picked up in intensity since

she'd gotten here. She had no idea how far away her car was. She'd been darn lucky to find the cabin. She shivered, her arms hugging her waist.

Finally, Leslie turned away from the window. She glanced at Jason and discovered him watching her.

"I'm going to have to stay here overnight," she finally said, more as a statement than a question.

"Looks like it, yeah."

She grasped her elbows tightly. "I don't have any clothes here."

"Not surprising. You wanted to use the phone, not move in."

She almost smiled. He had a succinct way of pointing out the obvious. Maybe the tension she'd been under for the past three days was warping her mind, but she didn't find him quite as intimidating as she had when she'd first met him. Just rude.

Of course, he could shoot her at any time, but somehow she didn't believe he would. She had a hunch he used his pistol for protection, not aggression. Leslie wondered if he needed protection from anyone in particular.

The thought was far from reassuring.

She looked down at what she was wearing and sighed.

He stood and made his way to the other end of the cabin. Over his shoulder he said, "I'll see what I have that you can sleep in."

She trailed after him and watched as he opened a large chest, pulled out some sweats, some sheets, pillowcases and blankets. "There are pillows on the bed," he said, nodding to the unmade bunks across from him.

"Thank you," she said, taking the proffered items. She quickly made up the lower bunk before she shook out the sweatshirt and pants. Even though she was tall, these would swallow her, but it couldn't be helped.

She turned and looked at him. "I hope you don't mind, but I was wondering if there was something to hang between us for a little privacy."

He looked at her as though she'd lost her mind. She didn't care what he thought. She folded her arms and refused to drop her gaze.

"I doubt that a blanket would give you privacy, unless you want to drape one from the top bunk. If that's what you want, be my guest."

He turned away and carefully retraced his steps to the other end. Just the little exertion had his leg throbbing. He went into the bathroom, closed the door and turned on the shower. He generally used a heating pad to relax the muscles in his thigh but with no electricity, the hot water was his only option. He was grateful that both the hot water heater and the kitchen stove ran on propane. He'd lucked out, getting to use this place. It had all the comforts of home. Except for the electricity going out periodically, he'd done fine here. Even had a stacked, apartment-size washer and dryer, as well as fully functional refrigerator and stove, and a pantry that he had heavily stocked so he wouldn't have to leave the place.

In addition, he had the room necessary for him to go through the excruciating physical therapy that would guarantee him the full use of his leg eventually.

By the time he finished his shower and redressed, Jase felt marginally better. He opened the door and stepped into the warm room, thankful to have enough wood chopped and stacked to keep the place heated until spring, with or without electricity. By then, he'd be rejoining his unit.

The thought was far from comforting. He still had nightmares from the attack, still felt tremendous guilt that he'd led his squad into an ambush, still fought the wish that he'd died along with the two that hadn't made it.

Leslie had rigged up two blankets, one on the side facing his bed, the other at the end of the bed. Since the bed sat in the corner of the cabin, the other two sides were protected from his leering view.

"Feel safer now?"

She turned to look at him. "Yes, thank you," she replied politely, her chin slightly raised. That chin of hers was a clear indication that she didn't intend to back down from him.

Despite himself, he was impressed. Not too many women he'd known would be handling the present situation without resorting to tears. He thought of his mother and smiled. And his oldest brother Jake's wife, Ashley. Now there were two women who stood up to whatever or whoever gave them grief, taking names and kicking butt.

He didn't know his other two sisters-in-law well enough to put them in the same category, but he had a strong hunch that any woman who would take on Jared and Jude would have to know how to stand her ground.

He went over to his chair and sat down. He'd been reading a biography of General Patton for the past few days. He found the man and his life to be fascinating. The bio had kept his mind off of his present circumstances. For a while, at least.

He needed to come to terms with his military career. He could ask for a discharge, but if he did, what would he do after that? He'd considered himself career military until that last recon mission. Despite the fact he'd been told by his superior officers several times in the hospital that there was nothing he could have done to save the two men's lives and that the rest of the squad, despite their wounds, survived because of his quick thinking, he had trouble accepting their reassurances. He shouldn't have lost a single man and he knew it.

"If you'll excuse me, I think I'll turn in. I was up rather early this morning." He looked up and saw that Leslie had changed into the sweats he'd given her. She had the pants doubled at the waist and they still puddled around her stockinged feet.

The sweatshirt was a little better. At least it should keep her warm.

Her determined politeness amused him for some reason. Gravely, he nodded his head. "I'll do my best not to make too much noise so as not to disturb you," he replied, equally politely. Since the only noise when they weren't talking was the sound of the wind howling and the occasional pop and sizzle of the wood inside the stove, he expected to get a smile out of her.

Instead she nodded soberly and returned to the other end of the room. He watched as she lifted a flap of the blanket and got into the bed, the blanket falling back into place and effectively concealing her.

He shook his head. You'd think the fact that he could barely get around would have convinced her she had no worries where he was concerned.

He wasn't certain whether to be flattered or insulted.

Two

"**T**ake cover! Take cover! Ambush! Thompson's hit. We've got to reach him! Nooooooooooo!"

Leslie sat straight up in bed, almost hitting her head on the bunk above. What was going on? Who was shouting?

She pulled the blanket back and saw that Jason must be dreaming. She could barely see that he lay on his bed without covers, wearing nothing but his underwear. He moaned and muttered something she couldn't quite decipher.

Slowly, Leslie released the blanket and lay down once again. What had happened to this man? Was he in the military? She turned over and faced the wall, pulling the covers up to her neck.

The room had cooled off considerably since she'd gone to bed and yet Jason lay bare. Maybe it was just as well that the room was so dark because she had seen more than she should have. The blanket around her bunk was to give him a little privacy, as well.

Leslie shivered. Wondering about the stranger whose cabin she was in kept her from worrying about her own situation. She didn't dare call Teri to see if those men had returned looking for her. With their access to law enforcement data, it was possible they had already discovered that she had rented a car.

Would they look for any relatives she might visit? If so, it was possible she may have endangered Larry and his family. Those men could already be in Michigan, looking for her.

The thought terrified her.

Eventually, Leslie drifted off to sleep. When she opened her eyes again a faint light in the room testified that morning had arrived. She pulled her arm out of the cover. The air was cold, although she could hear the crackling of the fire in the stove.

She sat up and pushed the blanket aside, surprised to see Jason on the floor near the stove, exercising. From his muttered curses, the movements must be painful and yet he continued to work his leg and, after several minutes, his arm and shoulders.

Leslie suddenly realized she was watching him once again without his knowledge and quickly dropped the blanket. The light from the kerosene lamp on the table had gilded his body, emphasizing the ridge of muscles running down his torso.

She waited until she heard the bathroom door close before she peeked out to make certain he was no longer in the main part of the cabin. When she knew she was alone, she hurriedly changed into her own clothes and folded the ones she'd borrowed and placed them on the pillow.

After warming her hands at the stove, she wandered into the kitchen nook and looked around. She was amazed at all the provisions. He didn't have much in the refrigerator but there was plenty of food for her to prepare for breakfast.

She quickly made a batch of biscuits, found some packages of dried fruit and nuts as well as oatmeal. While the biscuits cooked, she made oatmeal, adding dried apricots and chopped walnuts.

The table was set and coffee poured when Jason came out of the bathroom. He'd showered and shaved and she found the transformation remarkable, given the way he'd looked when she first arrived. He was younger than she'd guessed.

Once again he wore jeans and today had on a bulky sweater that must have been bought for him by a loved one because it matched the unusual color of his eyes.

He stopped abruptly when he saw the table. She ducked back into the alcove and grabbed the biscuits, quickly placing them on the table before returning to the kitchen.

"What—? You didn't have to—" He stopped when she returned with the oatmeal.

She smiled at him. "I hope you don't mind that I made breakfast."

"Mind?" he said slowly. He absently pulled her chair out for her before he sat. Ah, so he'd been taught manners at some time in his life—sometime before becoming a hermit. "Thank you," he said.

Neither one said anything during the meal. She replenished his oatmeal, finishing up what she'd made. When she set it in front of him, he looked up at her. "Where did you get the idea of putting stuff in the oatmeal?"

Since he'd wolfed down the first bowl, she didn't think he was criticizing her. She ate one of the biscuits while he finished off the rest of them. After sipping her coffee, Leslie replied, "That was one of my mother's ideas. I used to hate oatmeal so she started experimenting with different ingredients to coax me into eating it."

"Hmm. Where does your mother live?"

What had happened to the curmudgeon of the day before? The lines on his face were still there, especially around his mouth, but at least he was civilly attempting to make conversation.

"She lived in Alabama until she died last spring."

"I'm sorry to hear it. I bet you were raised in Alabama, weren't you?"

She frowned. "Yes. Why?"

He nodded. "Because your speech patterns sound like Alabama."

She tilted her head slightly. "And you know that because…?"

"One of the men in my squad was—" He stopped, shook his head and drank some coffee. The scowl on his face from yesterday returned.

She waited, but he said no more.

His squad. Military. Something bad had obviously happened that he didn't want to discuss. She could understand. She certainly had no intention of telling him why she'd left Tennessee in such a hurry.

She searched for another topic of conversation. Finally she said, "Are your parents still alive?"

He nodded and stood. He cleared the dishes from his side and carried them to the kitchen. She shrugged and finished clearing the table. When she went around the corner she saw that he was filling the sink with soapy water.

"I can do that," she said, adding the dishes she'd carried to the stack beside the sink.

"That's okay," he said without looking up. "Thanks for breakfast, by the way."

A clear dismissal.

She turned away with an inaudible sigh and went over to the stove, which was really radiating heat now. After holding her hands out to the warmth for a few minutes, she walked over to the window and looked out.

It was still snowing. Surprise, surprise. Maybe Jason hadn't been kidding about having snow until March. Surely the wind would let up soon. She watched the blowing snow for a while before turning away.

Now what?

She thought with longing about her belongings in the car. She'd bought several paperbacks and magazines on her way north, thinking she would need them once she reached Larry's place.

She needed them now.

With her decision made, Leslie grabbed her gloves and put on her coat, pulling the hood forward as far as it would go. Just as she reached for the door, Jason spoke.

"Where do you think you're going?"

The crabby curmudgeon had returned. Without turning around, she said, "To my car."

"Why?" he asked baldly.

She counted to ten. Slowly. Still facing the door she said, "Because I need some things out of it."

She heard his disgusted sigh. "You really love to court danger, don't you?"

Leslie shook her head. "As a matter of fact, I don't." She unlocked the door, opened it, quickly stepped through and slammed it behind her.

She looked around the area in front of her. She had no idea how to get back to the car the same way she came, but the clearing between the trees for his driveway was easy enough to see. She would walk that way until she came to the road, then follow the road until she reached her car.

With her plan complete, Leslie stepped off the porch into snow up to her knees. Great. Just what she needed. However, she had no intention of returning to the cabin without something to read, since it was obvious that her reluctant host didn't consider conversation with her necessary. She'd keep going if it killed her.

And it might.

Leslie lost track of time as she struggled to move through the snow. She had quickly learned to shuffle her way forward. Her legs were wet and clammy-cold. She clenched her teeth. She refused to go back and admit to Jason that he'd been right. So she continued forward, feeling like an inchworm.

By the time she reached the road, she was panting and she'd actually worked up a sweat, which was weird. The snow on the road wasn't as thick as the stuff on his driveway, probably because some of it had melted before the road cooled off.

She turned and looked back. The cabin was no longer in sight, but she saw the smoke rising, which encouraged her to believe she'd find her way back as she had yesterday.

The car was covered in snow when she found it still nestled in the ditch. Her winter gloves had been no match for the storm. The wool was soaked. She jerked them off and fumbled for the car keys she'd stuck in her coat pocket.

Leslie went to the trunk and pushed snow away until she found the lock.

It was frozen.

She didn't know whether to cry or to curse. She would not go back to the cabin without her belongings. With new determination she knelt until her mouth was close to the lock and began to blow on it. Every minute or so she'd jiggle the key before continuing to blow. She finally had to stop because she was getting light-headed and the back of her jaws ached from her efforts.

This time when she jiggled the key, there was a faint crunching sound and the key turned. She put all her muscle into prying open the trunk, feeling like a conqueror when it groaned open.

Not wasting any time, Leslie opened her suitcase, stuffed the various books and magazines scattered in the trunk into the bag, and pulled it out of the car.

She closed the trunk, grabbed her keys and looked around. She could either struggle back up the lane to Jason's house or she could cut through the trees, where the snow wasn't nearly as deep. There was no question which way she'd choose.

The way through the trees seemed much longer today than it had the day before, but then, she hadn't been dragging a suitcase the size of a pup tent at the time. Her mother had always told her she was too stubborn for her own good.

"You got that right, Mom," she said out loud. Maybe her mother had been there to help get the trunk open, knowing that Leslie wouldn't give up until it was open or she'd succumbed to the cold. She grinned at the thought.

She and her mom had always been close. Her mother

had been pregnant with her when her dad had been killed during a police action in the military twenty-six years ago.

Her mother had never been interested in another man and Leslie had grown up convinced that for every woman there was one particular male who was the right one for her. At the ripe old age of twenty-five, she wasn't as certain of that as she'd been at ten, though.

Her mother had made her feel very special, telling Leslie that she was so thankful she'd had her. She'd kept her husband's photos around the house so that Leslie would know who he was. What her mother probably hadn't considered was how much Leslie grew up despising all things military. She'd been deprived of a father; her mother deprived of a husband. And for what? Some military situation that was so minor in the general scheme of things as to have been long forgotten.

She paused and looked around her. It was darker beneath the trees but there was little underbrush to get in her way. She got a better grip on the handle of her suitcase and continued on, her thoughts going back to her childhood to a time when she wasn't alone, wasn't scared and wasn't half frozen.

She'd been gone for over an hour! Jason was so blasted angry at her that if she did manage to survive her outing, he just might strangle her himself.

He'd been pacing from window to window for the past twenty minutes, propelling himself around the room with the help of his cane. He hated feeling so helpless. Despite his wounded leg, he was much better prepared to survive out in this mess, so why hadn't he insisted on going himself?

Because he hadn't really believed she'd be so stupid as to go out there. He figured she'd stand out on the porch for a while, realize how ill equipped she was to make it and come back inside.

He didn't know how long he'd been reading when he realized she hadn't returned. With a curse, he'd gotten up and made his way to the door. When he'd opened it, he warmed the air with a blistering attack on her intelligence and her stubbornness. He could follow the trail she'd made until the driveway curved out of sight. The snow helpfully showed him how many times she'd fallen and gotten up, moved a few feet and fallen again.

She deserved to freeze out there. Or so he'd been telling himself for the past hour. Now he was scared. She'd been gone much too long. Like it or not, he was going to be forced to go find her, probably in a snowbank, unconscious.

He took the time to put on his heavy winter gear. He couldn't use the snowshoes, which further infuriated him. Instead he got his crutches out and hoped like hell he wouldn't fall while moving through the snow.

Jason had gone about ten feet down the driveway when a movement to his left caught his eye. It was Leslie, creeping along beneath the trees and pulling a humongous suitcase by a strap. Of course the thing tipped over, not for the first time from the looks of it, because the wheels couldn't work on this kind of terrain. Zombie-like, she stopped, righted it and crept on.

He wanted to shout all his fury at the universe for placing him in this situation. Instead he painstakingly turned and headed toward her.

She didn't see him until he was right in front of her and when she looked up, she screamed so loud that she startled him, throwing him off balance. If the crutches hadn't been planted so firmly, he would have toppled over backward.

"What the hell is wrong with you, woman? I came out to see if I could help!"

"You startled me," she replied, her voice a little hoarse.

"No kidding!" He reached over and lifted the suitcase. "Get into the house."

"But, I—"

"Go!" he thundered, causing her to jump. She stared at him and her look of terror almost undid him. He opened his mouth, closed it and finally said, "Please go into the house and get warm. I'll get this the rest of the way."

She nodded mutely and turned away. He watched her creep through the snow between them and the cabin, fall over, right herself and creep forward until she finally reached the porch. Only then did he hook the handle of the suitcase onto the crutch and hobbled forward.

When his nightmare finally ended and he placed the suitcase on the porch, Jase was exhausted. He'd had to rely on the damaged shoulder and it was telling him about it. His side felt as though he'd just run a 100K marathon and his thigh throbbed with each heartbeat.

His muscles were giving out on him when he finally reached the door. It opened just as he touched the handle and Leslie stared at him, wide-eyed.

"I'll get it," she said breathlessly, and pulled the suitcase inside. Then she turned back. "Let me help you—"

"Just get out of my way," he mumbled, too exhausted to raise his voice.

Once inside, he closed and locked the door and leaned against it, breathing hard, his eyes closed. When he finally opened them, she was standing in front of him, wringing her hands. "I'm so sorry. You shouldn't have gone after me. I was okay."

He stared at her for a long time. "Sure you were. Your lips are blue and you probably have hypothermia. Get those clothes off and get into the shower. Now." His voice was quite soft. He didn't know why she rushed away, dragging her suitcase.

She quickly opened it, throwing books and magazines everywhere, found some clothes and quickly went into the bathroom.

He had to get off his good leg or he wouldn't be able to get around at all. With painful movements he peeled off his winter garb and slowly made his way to his captain's chair near the potbellied stove.

He sat and carefully removed his boots before he leaned back in his chair.

What had happened out there? He'd been so blasted worried about her that the relief he'd felt when he'd spotted her had caught him off guard. Just because he didn't want her here didn't mean he wanted her to die.

Of course he'd been relieved at finding her determinedly dragging that mule train behind her, but what he'd felt at the time was much more than that.

And he didn't like it.

Three

Leslie stood underneath the warm water. She was so cold. She hadn't realized how cold until the water hit her skin. Although the water was barely warm, it hurt everywhere it touched her.

She stood with her eyes closed. Why had she done something so foolish? She had no answer.

She dreaded going back into the room where Jason waited. She'd never seen anyone as angry as he was. She worked for accountants who, by and large, were even-tempered people.

Her job! How could she have forgotten? She'd left without telling anyone, not even her boss. A tear trickled down her cheek. As if her whole life hadn't been turned upside down, she'd let her boss down.

Not that she could have told him what had happened or when she might be able to come back. The fact was that she might be running for the rest of her life. She'd have to find some kind of work, though, to survive. All her savings were tied up with her employee's benefit package. Sooner or later, she'd be forced to contact them.

Leslie finally turned off the water and stepped out of the shower. Compared to outside, the bathroom now felt almost toasty warm. Well, maybe not quite, but far better than what she'd felt outside.

Remembering her recent trek reminded her that Jason waited on the other side of the door. She shivered. It was a toss-up whether she was more afraid of freezing to death or of facing Jason's wrath.

At least she had clean clothes to put on. She'd grabbed the first things she could find. Now she understood why people wore long johns in the winter. Too bad she didn't have any. Once she got away from here, it would be the first item on her shopping list.

Jase forced his quivering arms to hold him as he went into the kitchen alcove. This was one time when he was going to break down and take the pain medication he'd been given.

He'd been trained to ignore pain and had elected not to take the meds because they made him feel weird, as if he was floating or half awake. At the moment he welcomed the sensation if it meant getting some relief.

After he swallowed them, Jase made more coffee, giving a silent plea for the electricity to return. He'd bought a top-of-the-line machine that could be programmed to make coffee. At the moment, his shaking hands spilled as much coffee as he managed to put into the campfire pot he'd found when he moved in. The old drip pot was better than nothing and he needed something hot. As did Leslie.

She'd turned off the shower several minutes ago but after that he'd heard nothing. He supposed he would hear some noise if she'd passed out and crashed onto the floor.

By the time the coffee was ready, the pain pills had taken the edge off and he managed to fill two cups and carry them to the table without spilling scalding coffee all over himself.

He heard the bathroom door open but he didn't look her way. "Have some coffee. It will help you get warm."

She didn't reply but he was damned if he was going to beg her to look after herself. She meant nothing to him. Less than nothing. Hell, he'd only known her for less than twenty-four hours.

He sipped on his coffee, keeping his eyes on the swirling snow, until she walked to the table and sat down. He glanced up at her and quickly away. She had a little color in her cheeks now and her lips were pinker.

"Thank you for coming out to help me," she said.

He lifted one shoulder in acknowledgment.

"You were right. I shouldn't have gone out there until the snow stopped. It was foolish and you have every right to be angry with me."

His head snapped up and he stared at her. "I'm not angry at you."

"You gave a great imitation, then."

"I was scared out of my wits, Leslie. You were gone much too long. I figured I'd find your body lying somewhere in a snowdrift."

A corner of her mouth lifted. "I couldn't get the trunk open. The lock had frozen."

"Then how did you get your bag?"

"I blew on it for what seemed like forever in hopes it would thaw a little." Before he could comment, she said, "I know. It was a stupid thing to do."

"Not if it worked." He settled back into his chair. Other than feeling as though he'd had several beers in quick succession, he felt fine. He glanced at her again. She looked like a baby chick with her fine hair in tufts around her face and neck. When she lifted her cup she saw him staring at her. She paused with her coffee halfway to her mouth and blinked.

She really was a cute kid. "How old are you?" he asked.

"Twenty-five."

"Really. I figured you to be in your teens."

"How old are you?"

"Just turned thirty." He could tell she was surprised. Probably thought he was some old crippled geezer. "How old did you think I was?"

"I didn't know. I'm not very good at judging people's ages."

"Ah." He waited, but when she didn't say anything more, he asked, "What do you do for a living?"

She placed her cup on the table, folded her hands around it and asked, "What difference does it make?"

"None whatsoever. Just making conversation."

"That's a change," she muttered, bringing her cup to her mouth and draining it.

"I realize I haven't been very friendly since you arrived."

"Gee. You think?"

He shrugged. "Okay, so I've been rude. I apologize. So why don't we start over?" He held out his hand. "Glad to meet you, Leslie O'Brien. I'm Jason

Crenshaw from Texas, and a member of the United States Army."

She tentatively reached out and took his hand. She was still cold, which was probably the reason electricity seemed to jump between them.

She took a deep breath and pulled her hand away. "I take it you're on leave of some kind."

"Medical leave. I'm considering getting out and doing something else. I have no idea what at the moment. Eventually, I'll be going home."

He wasn't looking forward to that visit. His only hope was to have his leg working well enough that he need never tell them that he'd been hurt.

"To Texas?"

He paused, wondering why he was talking about this. And to a stranger, at that. Who knew? If it helped her to be more comfortable around him, then why not? In a few days she'd be on her way to wherever she was going and he'd never see her again.

"Yeah, my folks have a ranch in Central Texas. In fact, it's been in the Crenshaw family since the 1840s."

"Wow," she whispered. "That's a long time."

He nodded. "I'm the youngest of four sons."

"The youngest? I would have thought you were the oldest, the way you act."

He grinned and she looked at him in amazement.

"What?" he asked.

"That's the first time I've seen you smile. You should do it more often."

He shook his head ruefully. "Sorry about that. I've been here on my own too long, I guess. Nothing much to smile at these past few months.

"As for my brothers, they don't give me much flak.

I went into the service right out of college. I rarely go home. Before this—" he gestured at his leg,"—I was out of the country most of the time. I stay in touch with them by e-mail."

"I bet they're worried about you, being hurt and alone up here."

"Nah. They don't know where I am or that I've been wounded. I plan to keep it that way." He looked around. "I don't know about you, but I'm hungry. Do you want some of the stew I made yesterday?" He started to push himself up.

"Please don't get up. I'll heat it up for us."

He watched her walk away from him. She certainly filled out those jeans nicely. These were khaki-colored, not the ones she wore yesterday. Her legs seemed to go on forever.

He knew she could hear him around the corner so he asked, "You haven't mentioned a husband or anyone who might be worrying about you. Is there someone you want to call on the cell phone?"

She leaned around the corner and looked at him for a long moment. "No. I'm not married and there's no-body worrying about me." She disappeared again.

"Oh. Too bad. You're a fine-looking woman, Leslie O'Brien, a fine-looking woman."

This time she came around the corner with her hands on her hips. "Have you been drinking?"

"No, ma'am."

"You're acting strange."

"Prob'ly the pills."

"What pills?"

"For pain."

She frowned. "They must be fairly strong."

"Who knows? I never take stuff like that."

"But you did today."

"Well, yeah. I was, uh, you know, uh, hurting a little more than usual."

"I see," she said, her frown intact.

"Why?"

She shook her head and disappeared. A few minutes later she brought them two bowls of stew, went back for two glasses of water, refilled their cups with coffee, then sat down.

"Maybe you'll feel better once you eat."

He picked up the spoon. "Oh, I'm feeling fine, just fine."

She grinned and he noticed she had a dimple in her cheek. "I'm beginning to believe that."

"That's the first time I've seen you smile. You have a dimple," he pointed out.

"That's right," she replied, chuckling for some reason, and began to eat.

He ate in silence. When he finished she asked, "Would you like some more?"

He shook his head. "Thanks, but no." When he tried to get up, she immediately took his dishes, along with her own, to the kitchen. With the help of one of the crutches, Jase made it to the big chair and sank down into it. He pushed the bar for the recliner and sighed with pleasure when his legs came up.

A few minutes later, Leslie came out of the kitchen area and looked surprised to see him sprawled in the chair. He waved his hand at the couch. "Here. Sit down. You need to rest."

She eyed him for a moment, then walked over and sat. "I thought I'd read."

"Oh. Well, I guess that's all right, if you don't want to talk."

Her lips twitched. "Actually, I'd rather listen to you."

He nodded agreeably. "Okay."

"Tell me more about your family."

His smile slipped. After a moment he said, "I love my family. My mom and dad are my heroes."

"Do you get along with your brothers?"

"Of course. Once they realized I wasn't taking anything off them, they learned to respect me. It's hell being the youngest," he added thoughtfully.

"I wouldn't know. I'm an only child."

"Too bad. Is your dad still alive?"

She shook her head. "He was killed in military action before I was born."

"Oh, man, that's rough."

"It was rougher on Mom. I never knew him, but she grieved for him, even though she worked hard to hide her pain from me." She deliberately changed the subject. "Are your brothers married or single?"

He burst out laughing. He couldn't help himself. "Would you believe that all three of my brothers, who swore they'd never get married, got married within a couple of years of each other? The first two were married only a couple of months apart."

"You're the lone holdout, I take it."

"You got that right. Besides, I've never had time to work on a relationship. I was determined to finish college in three years and get my commission."

"Are you saying you don't like women?"

"Nope. I'm saying I haven't had any time for women. Until now."

She stiffened. "What do you mean, now?"

He waved his hand airily. "Well, until my leg's strong enough to hold me and I go back to my unit, I've got all the time in the world to do anything I want."

"Is that why you're hiding up here in the woods?"

Hmm. Maybe she had a point. With all the time in the world, why was he staying by himself? Oh, yeah, because he didn't want his family to see him like this. He didn't want them to worry about him. He didn't want to bring his guilt and anger and frustration home to them.

"I didn't want to see or talk to anybody. I led my squad into an ambush and two men were killed. I should have died with them."

"Looks like you almost did."

"I know. Guess it wasn't in the cards for me."

"You sound disappointed."

"I've asked to be reassigned. No more combat. They'll either put me behind a desk or have me train others."

"Sounds like a way for you to use your skills."

After several minutes of silence, Jase murmured, "I'm tired."

"Oh, well, why don't you try to rest? I'll just get one of my books and—"

"No, I don't mean tired right now. I've been in the army for nine years, working in special ops. I was good at it. But I screwed up that night. I should have double-checked, hell, triple checked, the info we received to make sure what we had was accurate. I don't want that kind of responsibility again."

"I think you're being a little hard on yourself."

He shrugged. "Doesn't matter, anyway."

"Do you intend to let your family know what happened?"

"Not if I can help it, no. I want to be in good physical condition the next time I see them." He closed his eyes. "I'm ashamed to face them, all right? I wanted them to be proud of me and what I've accomplished. I don't want them to know that I screwed up."

"I have a hunch they'll be too glad you survived to care about anything else and, from what you've told me, I doubt they'll believe you screwed up. I know I don't."

He opened his eyes. "You're a nice person, Leslie O'Brien."

"Yep. Nice. That's me."

"Do you have a boyfriend?"

She laughed. "Why are you so interested in my personal life?"

"Well, we talked about mine. I think. Didn't we?"

"I date once in a while. Nothing serious."

"Good."

She raised her brows. "Good?"

He closed his eyes. "Yeah," he said, drawling his words, "'cause I don't want to be stepping on anybody's toes."

Four

Leslie couldn't believe what she was hearing. She stiffened in outrage at his cavalier attitude toward her. She wanted to say something cutting, something belittling, in response, something that wouldn't betray the way his words had affected her.

He didn't stir. She stood and looked closer at him. He lay there bonelessly sprawled in his chair. He had thick lashes she'd never noticed before, probably because his eyes had always drawn her complete attention.

Jason's hair fell across his forehead and she wanted to push it gently back, but she restrained herself.

He made a sound and at first she thought he'd said something until she realized he was asleep and the soft noise she'd heard was his deep breathing.

She turned away and spotted her suitcase in the middle of the floor between their beds, paperbacks and magazines scattered around it. How could she have forgotten to pick those up?

She made a neat stack of them, found her warmest pair of pajamas and laid them at the foot of her bed. She also dug out socks because her feet had gotten cold the night before.

Sometime while they were talking, the light had disappeared outside. She glanced at her watch and was surprised to see that it was almost eight o'clock.

My, how time flies when your reluctant host is busy making passes at you.

What a strange day this had been. She wondered if Jason would remember talking to her and revealing so much about himself. Would he resent her for being the one who'd listened to his pain?

She glanced over her shoulder. He looked comfortable where he was. She looked around the room and saw that the stove needed more wood. There was a huge stack on the porch so she quietly put on her coat, opened the door and hauled several pieces inside.

Next, she put them in the stove as she'd watched him do, and quietly closed the small door of the efficient heat source.

He didn't stir.

Leslie went to the table and blew out the lamp before she slipped behind the blanket around her bed. Once she'd dressed for bed, she went into the bathroom and brushed her teeth.

When she came out of the bathroom, she looked over at him. He hadn't moved. She found an extra blanket and draped it over him, tiptoed to her bed and slipped in between the covers.

Despite her exhaustion, Leslie had trouble falling

asleep. She'd never known a man like Jason. He was troubled, but who wouldn't be, having gone through what he had.

She reminded herself that he was exactly the kind of man she'd vowed never to become involved with: a military man.

Not that his career really mattered. Once she left, she knew there would be no reason for her ever to see him again. At least she had a different opinion of him now that she'd gotten to know him a little better. Pain would explain his rude and irascible behavior.

If she were home, she'd probably be across the hall from her apartment visiting with Teri and discussing the mixed emotions this man caused her.

Teri.

She prayed that Teri was all right.

The grating sound of metal rubbing against metal woke her up and she realized the noise she heard was the old recliner as it straightened. Impulsively, Leslie slipped out of bed to check on him.

"Jason?"

The silence lengthened until he finally said, "Sorry to wake you," in a gruff voice.

"Is there something I can do for you?"

Another pause. "No. I'm going to put more wood in the stove and go to bed."

Because of the moonlight coming through the window, she could see him sitting in the chair, holding his head. She carefully made her way over to the sofa.

"The storm's over," she said softly.

"Yeah. I think it was the silence after listening to the wind for the past couple of days that woke me up."

She sat on the edge of the couch, close enough to touch him. "Are you in pain?"

The strangled noise he made sounded like coughing, choking and chuckling. "I've felt better. I guess the meds must have worn off." After a moment he said, "I must have talked your ear off earlier. I apologize."

"No apology needed. I enjoyed it."

"I've talked more in the past two days than I have in the past three months."

"Sometimes it helps." She reached over and touched his arm. He stiffened. What was she thinking? She'd wanted to comfort him in some way and had stepped over an invisible line between them.

When she started to pull her hand away, he placed his hand over it, trapping her fingers. "You startled me. It's been a long time since anyone has touched me."

Amused, she said, "That's not all that surprising, is it, considering your hermit status."

"Hermit, huh?"

"I thought that sounded better than curmudgeon."

"Are you actually insulting your host after I saved you from the storm?" He hadn't moved his hand from hers. He slid his fingers between hers and squeezed gently.

"Rather rude of me, I know," she replied, embarrassed that she sounded a little breathless.

"When was the last time *you* were touched?" he murmured.

She tried to pull her hand away but stopped when he tightened his grip. "It's been a long time," she admitted.

Leslie lost track of time as they sat in silence with their hands clasped. Finally, Jason sighed and released her. "I need to get that wood before it gets any colder in here."

"I'll do it," she said quickly, and stood. She moved to the coatrack and felt for her coat. Once it was fastened, she opened the cabin door and stepped outside.

The snow lay in large drifts, sparkling in the moonlight. The unexpected beauty took her breath away. She'd had no idea what a lovely decoration a blanket of snow could be.

She gathered the wood and went back inside at the same time Jason came out of the bathroom. He moved slowly toward her, leaning heavily on his cane.

"Here, let me take that," he said.

"I can do it. I added some logs earlier while you were asleep." She dropped the logs on the floor near the stove, removed her coat and hung it back on its peg. When she turned, he was already replenishing the stove.

"Where were you injured?" she asked quietly when he straightened with a muffled groan.

"You mean, where was I when it happened?"

She chuckled. "No. I meant your wounds. I know your leg must have been injured."

"I got hit in the shoulder, side and thigh. The doctors told me that I was lucky that none of the bullets hit a vital organ. The muscles and tendons in my thigh are taking more time to heal than I like, though. I don't trust my leg to hold my full weight yet. They told me that eventually I'd be able to walk without a limp." He straightened and turned toward her. "Except when the weather changes, my shoulder and side don't bother me much." He frowned. "And I don't know why in the hell I'm telling you all this."

They stared at each other for a moment before he turned away and went over to his bed. He sat and carefully pulled off his boots, socks and jeans. Next he pulled his sweatshirt over his head, leaving him in his T-shirt and briefs.

"Are you going to bed?" he asked, sounding impatient.

She nodded, but wasn't sure he could see her. "Yes."

She lifted the edge of the blanket and took a step when he said, "Leslie?"

She turned. "Yes?"

"Are you afraid of me?"

"Not at all."

"Then take the blanket down. It blocks the heat from reaching you."

Feeling foolish, she tugged on the blanket until it fell into her arms.

"I would never take advantage of you," he said softly. "Please believe me."

She turned and looked at his shadowy figure. "I do." She spread the blanket on top of the others on her bed.

"Leslie?"

She smiled to herself. The meds must still be working some, whether they blocked the pain or not, because he was continuing to be so verbal. "Yes?"

There was a long pause. "Never mind."

"May I get you something?"

"No," he replied tersely. "Forget about it."

She walked over to him and knelt beside his bed. "Tell me, Jason."

He sighed. "I was thinking that we could stay warmer if we shared a bed. I told you it was stupid." He lifted the covers and stretched out beneath them. "Good night," he said abruptly.

"Jason?"

"What!"

"Do you want me to sleep with you?" She was extremely glad he couldn't see her embarrassment or that her pulse rate had shot into triple digits.

"I'm in no condition to do more than hold you," he added wryly.

Leslie straightened out of her kneeling position. Slowly she said, "All right." Unless she started to hyperventilate first.

She sat beside him on the side of the bed. This was a first for her. She'd never slept with anyone before, male or female. And in a bunk bed?

Their earlier conversation must have brought back some painful memories for him; otherwise she knew he would never have asked her to do this.

She glanced at him and saw that he had shifted so that his back was now against the wall.

Should she face him? The bed was too narrow for her to lie on her back. He overcame her hesitation by wrapping his arm around her waist and pulling her toward him, causing her to tumble into the bed next to him, spoon fashion.

"Is this okay?" he asked gruffly.

She felt as though she were cuddled next to a furnace. Only then did she realize how cold she was. She sighed, releasing the breath she hadn't been aware of holding.

"It's fine," she whispered.

"Good." He kept his arm around her waist. Tentatively she placed her arm next to his.

They lay there in silence; Leslie's every muscle tensed. Finally he said, "Somehow I get the impression you're not used to this."

She swallowed. "You're right. Being an only child meant I had a room—and a bed—to myself."

"No sleepovers with your friends?"

"Not that we shared a bed."

"Does this make you uncomfortable?"

She thought about his question. "A little." She forced herself to relax. "Maybe not uncomfortable, exactly. Just a little strange."

He yawned. "Good night," he said, his breath caressing the back of her neck and his voice drifting off.

Leslie closed her eyes, feeling his warmth from her head to her toes, and with another big sigh, drifted off to sleep.

Jason surfaced from a deep sleep to discover there was a woman in his bed. What the—? He raised his head and saw Leslie O'Brien sound asleep beside him.

He jerked his hand away from her breast and attempted to move away, but the bed was too narrow and his back was against the wall.

He vaguely recalled asking her to sleep with him the night before. He must have been out of his mind. His body already knew exactly what it wanted to do with the woman so conveniently tucked against him, her rounded bottom nestled against a painful erection.

He looked around the room and realized that the electricity had come back on. He thought he'd turned off the light over the table. Guess he was wrong.

Leslie stirred. He pulled back as far from her as possible in their narrow confines, which he quickly discovered wasn't one of his better ideas because he'd given her room to roll onto her back and stretch. He waited for her to open her eyes and scream bloody murder. Instead she slowly opened them, saw him and gave him a sleepy smile that almost undid what little composure he had left.

"Good morning," she said softly, touching his face with her hand. "Did you sleep all right or did I crowd you?"

Her fingers were warm against his unshaven face. Not even a saint could resist this woman first thing in the morning. He leaned toward her and gently touched her lips with his, half expecting her to shove him away.

Once again, he was wrong. She lifted her mouth to his in an innocent response that curled his toes.

He ran his tongue across the seam of her lips and she obligingly opened her mouth. The kiss went on and on until Jason knew he had to stop *right now* because he had told her the absolute truth. He was in no shape to make love to her, despite his desperate need to slip deep inside her.

He forced himself to pull away and stared at her. Her face was flushed with more than sleep now and her slightly swollen mouth glistened from their intense kiss.

"I need to get up," he said roughly.

"Oh! I'm sorry," she replied, and quickly got out of bed.

For the first time since she'd arrived, Jason wished for a privacy blanket of his own. He grabbed the closest one, wrapped it around his waist and slowly worked his way out of bed. Thankfully she'd turned away and was digging into her mammoth bag. She had enough clothes in there to last for weeks.

He grabbed his cane and headed to the bathroom and a shower. Better yet, he should probably open the cabin door and throw himself into the closest snowbank.

Once under the shower, Jason thought about the past two days. Leslie O'Brien had entered his life and turned it upside down. He looked back over the past few months and realized that he no longer wanted to hibernate. Now that she'd appeared in his life, he had no desire to continue nursing his wounds, both physical and emotional.

For the first time since she'd knocked on his door he wondered where Leslie had been headed when her car had gone into the ditch. Suddenly he wanted to know everything about her—who she was and how she'd become the gentle soul she was today.

As soon as he dried off and dressed, he intended to find out.

Leslie was in a great mood. She'd awakened a couple of times during the night and had felt warm and protected.

She smiled at the memory. She'd finally become toasty warm for the first time since her car had gone off the road. She felt deliciously wicked, sleeping with a man. She wondered where she'd found the courage to say yes.

Leslie began dressing and realized that there was a light glowing over the table. The electricity had come on sometime during the night.

She pulled on one of her favorite sweaters. Her mother had given it to her last Christmas. She'd told her that the amber color matched her eyes. Leslie knew that her father'd had the same color eyes. She dug around for her navy-blue woolen slacks, added thick socks to her ensemble and padded into the kitchen.

She would make pancakes this morning. She hummed while she worked, and her thoughts kept darting back to the kiss she'd shared with Jason.

A good-morning kiss was a great way to start the day.

By the time Jason came out of the bathroom—cleanly shaved—she had breakfast on the table.

"Are you ready to eat?" she asked.

"Just a sec. I need to get dressed."

She turned away and found something to do in the kitchen. He deserved some privacy, after all.

When he came to the table she had to look away quickly before she gave herself away. She loved the scent of his aftershave and the way his sandy-colored hair curled around his ears and nape of his neck. And his rare smile made her knees weak.

She wondered if she'd be so attracted to any man with whom she'd slept. It was hard to imagine. Her entire body tingled whenever she looked at him.

"This looks delicious," he said, lowering himself into his captain's chair. "Keep this up and I'm going to be spoiled, wanting breakfast waiting for me every morning."

She blushed. "Thank you," she said quietly, and sat across from him.

They were almost through with breakfast when Leslie heard a loud sound coming from the road. Her sense of well-being vanished. "What's that noise?" she asked, hating that her voice quivered.

Jason paused and listened, then continued to eat. He washed the bite down with coffee, then said, "Snowplow. Looks like they're opening up the roads."

"Oh." She swallowed. Reality had intruded. "Then I can call someone to get my car out of the ditch."

"You can call, but there's no telling how long it will take for someone to get out here. I'm sure you aren't the only one who has a stuck vehicle. I hate to rain on your parade, but with the amount of snow we got, the snowplow will bury your car. The snow has to go somewhere. Have you ever seen them blow snow?"

She shook her head.

She forced herself to calm down. There was really no need for her to panic. Those men, even if they'd found out she was in a rental car, wouldn't be able to find her up here. She'd made certain there wouldn't be a paper trail for them to follow.

"Looks like you may be stuck with me for a while longer, then," she said lightly.

He took the last bite of his pancakes and seemed to savor it, if his blissful expression was any indication, before he replied, "I'll try to live with my disappointment." He laughed when he saw the expression she hadn't been able to hide. What had she expected? Of course he wanted her gone. She'd imposed on his hospitality too long as it was. "I'm kidding, Leslie! I'm not in any hurry to see you leave. I enjoy your company."

"You do?"

"Yes, ma'am, I certainly do. By the way, do you have any interest in cards? We could play a few games to pass the time, if you'd like."

"I played cards with Mom when I was a child, but I doubt that you'd be interested in playing Old Maid or Go Fish." He looked disappointed. "We also played gin rummy once I was older."

"Great! We'll play that. And I might teach you how to play poker, if you're interested."

"Poker? Isn't that a betting game?"

"We can use matches for money."

"Oh. I guess that would be all right." She stood and cleared the table, and was surprised to see him follow her.

"Are you feeling better this morning?" she asked, filling the sink with soap and water.

He leaned against the counter. "Yes and no."

She glanced at him. "That's definitive."

"I probably got my best night's sleep since I left the hospital."

"From the pain medication, right?"

"Maybe, but I discovered that I sleep much better with you in my arms."

Oh, my. She knew she must have turned fire-engine red. What was she supposed to say to that?

She cleared her throat. "Glad I could be of help." She concentrated on scrubbing dishes.

"While I was in the shower, I was thinking about all the talking I've been doing and realized that you've said very little about yourself. I know you were raised by your mother, who passed away, and that you work for a firm of accountants."

She forced herself to look at him and did her best to smile. "That pretty much sums up my life. I went to school, made decent grades, graduated from college and accepted the first job offered to me. I've been there ever since."

"I'm curious, though. What would cause a Southern belle like you to decide to come to Michigan at this time a year?"

What could she say? She didn't want to lie. He might accept the truth. Of course he would accept the truth. She just had a difficult time even thinking about what happened, much less discussing it.

She wiped the counter down and turned to him.

"I suppose that I could—" She paused. "Does the snowplow clear your drive for you?"

"No. I'll have to hire someone to do that. Why?"

"Because I heard something." She glanced through the window and ducked to the floor. It was them! They'd found her, after all. What could she do? Where could she hide?

"Leslie, are you okay? What did you trip on?"

"N-nothing. T-those men in that c-car. T-they're looking f-for m-m-me. I, uh, came up here h-hoping they wouldn't discover w-where I'd gone." She crawled past the window and jumped to her feet. She ran to her bed and pulled the covers off, looked around wildly and saw his trunk sitting there. She shoved the bedding inside. Then she grabbed her suitcase and pushed and shoved it under his bed. When she stood and turned, he was looking at her as though she'd lost her mind.

Well, she was close to it, that was certain.

"I'm going to hide in the bathroom because it's the only place I can think of. Please, please don't let them inside. They can't find me! Please help me."

He blinked. "Sure." He glanced around the room. "No sign of anyone besides me here."

She darted into the bathroom and hid between the sink cabinet and the tub. Whether she tried to hide in the tub or right there, if they came looking for her in here, they'd immediately see her.

She'd deliberately left the door ajar so that anyone looking would see that it was an unoccupied bathroom. Plus she wanted to hear what was said.

Leslie waited in that uncomfortable position for what seemed like an interminable amount of time, following their progress up the driveway by the sound of crunching snow. Thank goodness the drive hadn't been plowed or they would have been here before she could have moved fast enough.

She finally heard stamping feet on the porch accompanied by a brisk knock.

From her limited view she could see that Jason had picked up his pistol before going to the door.

"Who is it?" he asked brusquely.

"Police."

Five

The police! What the—?

Jason whipped his head around and stared at the bathroom door, which stood ajar. What was going on here? Why would the police be looking for Leslie? What had she done?

Somehow he had a hunch this wasn't about an overdue parking ticket.

He quickly slipped his pistol beneath his sweater at the small of his back, unlocked and opened the door. The sun bouncing off the snow almost blinded him.

He squinted at the two men standing on the porch, both wearing uniforms and dark sunshades. Not that he could blame them for the glasses. He looked them over. One was tall and trim, about thirty-five; the other was shorter, and the little hair he had left was gray. They each held out badges for him to see. Jason took his time, looking at the photos and comparing them to his visi-

tors. The tall one was Leonard Cowan and the other
Bryce Denton.

According to their IDs, they were deputy sheriffs
from Deer Creek, Tennessee. Wherever the hell that
was. Leslie had told him when she arrived that she was
from Tennessee. He didn't understand why she'd panicked when she'd seen them, though. As far as he could
tell, they were who they said they were.

He didn't like the idea that she was hiding from the
police.

Jason stood in the doorway without inviting them
inside.

"Can I help you?" he finally asked, feeling mystified
by their sudden appearance.

Leonard answered. He had a deep, soothing, almost
reassuring voice. "We hope so. We're looking for an escaped prisoner. Have you seen this woman?"

Jason stared at a grainy photograph of Leslie. She
was an escaped prisoner? No wonder she didn't want
these men to find her! After carefully studying the
photo, he handed it back. "'Fraid not. I don't get visitors, especially in the winter. What's she charged with?"

Bryce answered. "Doesn't matter. We need to find her."

Leonard smiled at Jason. "We're just trying to do
our job."

"What makes you think she's in Michigan? According to those IDs, you're from Tennessee. Where did she
escape from?"

Bryce snapped, "We're not here to answer questions,
buddy. We're looking for answers."

What an obnoxious ass. Jason shrugged, feeling a little better about lying to them. "Sorry. Like I said, I
don't get visitors here. Guess I forgot my manners."

Leonard said, "If she happens to show up, give us a call. We have reason to believe she's in this area." He handed Jason his card. "That's my cell number. You can reach me there at any time, day or night."

"Sure, although I can't see why anyone would hightail it to Michigan from Tennessee. She must have done something pretty serious to come north at this time of year."

Instead of answering him, the men turned and stepped back into the snow, cursing as it clung to their pant legs. Jason shut the door, locked it and waited by the door until the engine started. He heard the sound of spinning wheels and crossed over to the window. Staying out of their line of sight, he watched as the car refused to move forward, so that the driver had to back out, following the tracks he'd made earlier.

Jason waited until he could no longer hear them. If they were suspicious of him for any reason they might decide to come back on foot, but somehow he doubted it. He was surprised they'd found his driveway after the snowplow had come through, although he had noticed in the past that the road crew attempted not to block private driveways.

Those two men were as out of place here as Leslie was. Speaking of which… He headed to the other side of the cabin and pushed on the bathroom door until it swung open all the way.

She was huddled between the sink cabinet and the tub with her head buried in her knees. Her entire body shook.

He studied her. If he had gotten to know her at all, he knew this was no act. The woman was scared to death—and he intended to find out why. Right now.

"What a surprise to find that you're a fugitive from the law, Leslie. I would never have guessed. How about telling me what the hell is going on? I need to know what kind of trouble I'm in for aiding and abetting a criminal."

She couldn't breathe. Her chest hurt and she needed air, but she could not breathe! She felt his arms on her shoulders and she looked up at him.

"You look like you're about to pass out," he said impatiently. "Come back in here and talk to me."

She wasn't certain her knees would hold her but she forced herself to stand. Jason had turned away to leave, which was a good thing because she proceeded to lose her breakfast. By the time she finished, she was on her knees again.

He startled her by handing her a damp cloth. Nothing like total humiliation to strengthen her backbone. She took the cloth without looking at him, rubbed her mouth and stood once again. She splashed water in her face and rinsed her mouth before she looked at him.

"Thanks," she said, not sure whether she meant for the cloth or for lying for her.

He went over to the kitchen and poured each of them a cup of coffee. He handed her one after dumping some sugar into it and took his to the table.

"Sit," he said, nodding his head toward her chair. She did and immediately sipped the coffee. She made a face. "If you'd rather have tea, go ahead and make it. You're in shock and you need the sugar."

Jase wondered why he was so concerned about her. Hadn't he realized this morning in the shower that he didn't know anything about her? Those men had brought that home to him. He intended to get some answers.

"Were you caught embezzling?"

She shook her head.

"Then what? Don't play games with me, damn it. I want to hear your story. I want to hear all of your story, and I want you to tell me the truth."

She drank the coffee as though it was medicine, shuddering when she finished it. He watched as she set the cup aside, clasped her hands and began to talk.

Leslie had worked late on that terrible Friday night since she'd had no plans for the evening and she was behind in her work. She hadn't left her office building in downtown Deer Creek until almost nine.

The parking lot was practically deserted and she'd had to walk across it to get to her car. She'd been late to work that morning—another reason she'd decided to work late—and couldn't find a parking space close to the building. Her car was parked by a Dumpster half hidden by a willow tree that concealed her car.

As she'd neared her car, she spotted two cars at the back of the parking lot with three men standing nearby, talking. Always nervous about being alone at night, she'd picked up her pace, glad she'd slipped off her pumps and replaced them with her sneakers before leaving the office. The rubber soles had muffled her steps. None of them looked around and she'd hurried to her car, glad that she'd had to park in such an out-of-the-way place.

She had almost reached her car when she'd heard a strange popping noise. She'd glanced over at the three men to see one of them fall to the ground. The tall man had held some kind of gun with a long barrel in his hand. He'd motioned for the other man to pick up the man who'd been shot.

Leslie hadn't believed what she'd seen. She'd reached her car and carefully opened the door. Once inside, she'd carefully shut it and punched the lock for all of the doors.

She'd broken out into a cold sweat. Oh, my God. She'd witnessed a killing. She had to get away from there and call the police. She'd started the car and immediately pulled away. She'd heard a shout. Glancing into her rearview mirror she'd seen one of the men chasing after her. She'd pressed her foot into the floorboard and her car jumped ahead, racing down the street.

Where were the police when she needed them? Couldn't they pull her over for speeding?

Car lights had hit her mirror and she'd seen one of the cars from the parking lot coming up behind her, fast. She'd driven faster despite the fact that he was flashing his high and low beams as a signal to stop.

There was no way she'd ever stop for killers!

As soon as the street curved, she'd spun the wheel and turned into a residential area. She'd thought she'd lost him when he swung around the corner behind her. She'd turned again and again, turning off her lights, although she'd known her brake lights would give her away. If she could only get far enough away to lose him. She pulled onto yet another street. Praying that she could pull this off—she'd seen it done in a movie once—Leslie had turned a corner sharply, pulled into a driveway, driven up next to the house into deep shadows and stopped.

The car had passed but in a few minutes was back, moving much slower. She'd slid down in her seat. Why hadn't she gotten out and run while she'd had the chance? It was too late. If he found her, she had no hope of surviving the night.

She'd waited for what felt like hours but the car didn't come back. She'd waited some more. This could be a trick if he knew for sure that she'd turned down this street.

But maybe he didn't. Maybe she could get across town to her apartment complex without him spotting her. After all, neither of the men in the parking lot had any idea who she was. She prayed that it was too dark for them to have seen her license plate number.

Once home, she'd be safe.

Leslie had never felt such relief as she did when she'd pulled into her small apartment complex. There were eight apartments: four up and four down. Rather than park her car where it could be spotted from the street—she hadn't wanted to take any chances of being found—she parked at the rear of the complex on the edge of the parking area.

She'd raced upstairs to her apartment and let herself in. She'd looked at the clock. Almost ten-thirty. So much had happened in such a short time that she'd thought it was two or three in the morning.

Leslie had called the sheriff's office and explained what she'd seen. The dispatcher got her name and address and said he would send a couple of deputies to interview her.

Now that she'd notified authorities, Leslie was on edge. Her neighbor, Teri, who lived across the hall from her, was probably watching television since her husband was out of town this week.

She'd hurried across the hall and tapped on the door. When Teri, yawning and tying her robe, opened her door, Leslie had felt awful for waking her up.

"I'm so sorry, Teri. I'll talk to you tomorrow."

"No, wait! I'm awake now. What's happened? You look like you've seen a ghost."

Leslie hadn't known what to do. She hadn't wanted to bother her friend and neighbor, but she hadn't want to sit in her apartment alone waiting for the deputies to arrive.

"I, uh, I saw something tonight that I shouldn't have seen and I'm afraid."

Teri had grabbed her hand and pulled her into the apartment. The only light came from a streetlamp shining through the window. Leslie had sunk onto the sofa and hugged her knees to her chest.

Teri had sat across from her. "What? What in the world has happened?"

"I saw a man shot and killed tonight."

"Oh, my gosh! Where? Where were you? Where was he?"

Leslie had given her a quick sketch of what she'd witnessed. When she'd finished, Teri asked, "Could you identify the men?"

"Yes, the parking lot was well lit. And one of them followed me in a car and I kept getting glimpses of him from the overhead streetlights."

"Did you recognize him?"

Leslie had shaken her head. "I could swear I've never seen any of the men before tonight. The man who was killed had red hair. He wasn't very tall, maybe my height, and was slender. The shorter guy picked him up as though he weighed next to nothing. I left after that and the other one chased me all over town."

"You're lucky you got home okay. Are you sure you weren't followed?"

"I'm not sure of anything anymore."

Teri had stood and said, "Let me fix you some tea. You say the deputies are on their way?"

Leslie'd nodded. "I've got to stay calm and sound rational when they ask for a statement and descriptions. I don't want to come across as some hysterical female with a wild imagination."

"Honey, you have a right to get hysterical, and don't you forget it."

Leslie remembered sitting by the window to watch for the deputies. She'd been scared to death, but once she told them what she'd seen, it would be in their hands. After that she would have police protection and could lead a normal life.

Teri had arrived with two cups of tea and sat in a chair nearby. They were silent as they sipped the aromatic tea. Slowly, Leslie had begun to relax.

"I've never witnessed anything like that," she'd finally said to break the silence. She'd shivered. "I hope I never see anything like it again."

She'd glanced back at the window to see the patrol car pulling into the complex. "There they are," she'd said with a sense of relief. "I need to get back to my apartment so they won't think—" As she'd watched the deputies get out of the car, Leslie fully grasped the danger she was in.

"Are you telling me that you saw one of the men who was just here shoot somebody?" Jason asked.

She nodded her head. "I couldn't see them from the bathroom, but I recognized their voices from when I heard them talking to Terri. They were the men I saw in the parking lot." Her teeth were chattering from nerves. They had found her, despite everything she had done.

She saw the disbelief in Jason's eyes and closed her

eyes. He didn't believe her and he had the number of the deputy. He could call him at any time and what could she do to stop him?

Leslie glanced at the piled snow on the other side of the window and knew she had no way to escape.

"Is that why they arrested you?" he finally asked. "On some trumped up charge?"

She shook her head. "They never saw me again. What they told you was a lie." Now he would be forced to decide who was lying. She opened her eyes and looked at him. He was studying her and she knew what he must be thinking.

Or thought she did, until he said, "That's good to know, although I wouldn't have blamed you if you *had* done everything in your power to get away from them."

The tension left her, leaving her limp. For whatever reason, Jason had decided to believe her.

He put his arm around her and hugged her to him. "It's going to be okay, you know."

"Not if they've followed me clear up here. I have no place else to go."

"I'm curious how you managed to get away from them. What did you do after you realized who they were?"

She attempted a smile. "I panicked. What else? I had counted on giving them my statement and going on with my life as though nothing had happened. Now, because of my phone call, I'd told them who I was and where I lived."

"Couldn't you have gone to the city police?"

"The town's too small to have its own police department. The sheriff's office is the law enforcement in the county."

"Does the sheriff know about this?"

"I have no idea. I certainly wasn't going to hang around and make another phone call to find out." Her head rested on his shoulder. He had a firm grip on her and his body heat slowly warmed her.

After a brief silence Jason asked, "Tell me what you did next."

"If it hadn't been for Teri, I wouldn't have made it this far. She told me to go into her bedroom and close the door and let her handle them. We listened as they came up the steps. They knocked on my door. Then they knocked again. Finally, they were pounding on the door and calling my name."

Because she was in her nightclothes, Teri went to her door and, keeping the chain on, opened it enough to see them.

"What's the matter with you people?" she demanded. "Don't you know we're trying to sleep around here?"

One of them said, "We got a call from Ms. O'Brien reporting a crime. She said she'd meet us here so we could get all the particulars."

Teri unlocked the door and opened it. "Well, she must not be here or she'd have answered the door. No one could sleep through that racket."

"She has to be here. The call came from her phone."

"Really? Do you think somebody broke into her apartment?"

One of them looked at the other. "We better check it out."

Teri said, "I have her extra key. We traded in case of an emergency. This certainly sounds like an emergency. I hope my husband managed to sleep through this. If not, I have to go tell him what's going on."

Leslie hadn't closed the bedroom door all the way but the room was pitch-black and she knew they couldn't see her. She stepped back when Teri walked in and closed the door behind her.

"How did I do?"

"If I didn't know better, I would have believed you myself. What are you going to do now?"

"Why, let Deer Creek's finest into your apartment. We'll have a look around, I'll point out that nothing appears to be disturbed, and I'll get rid of them."

Which is exactly what Teri did. Leslie listened as they tromped down the stairs and returned to the patrol car. Teri joined her at the bedroom window and they watched the car drive away.

"It worked," Leslie said.

"Yeah, for the moment. Now we have to get you out of town. Do you have a place to go where they won't think to look? They aren't going to stop until they find you. They can't afford not to find you."

It took a few minutes for Leslie to think clearly enough to go through her list of family members. "I have a cousin, Larry, who lives in Grand Rapids, Michigan. He and his wife have a summer cottage on one of the lakes there."

Teri quickly dressed. "Good. Call him, while I go hunt you up some transportation."

"Oh, you've done enough, Teri. I'll take the bus into Nashville and fly to Grand Rapids."

"Exactly what they'll expect you to do. Look, honey, these guys mean business. They'd be waiting for you when you stepped off the plane. There's no reason for you to leave a trail for them to follow. Ed down at the garage rents cars sometimes and he lives behind the shop. Tell him you need a car for a few days because of an emergency. Ed's not officially licensed as a car rental agency, so he won't be on most lists those slime balls might check."

Once Teri left, Leslie slipped across the hall into her own apartment. Without turning on any lights, she hurried to her bedroom, thankful for the night light that came on automatically at dusk, and grabbed her mother's old suitcase. She opened drawers and began to throw clothes on the bed. It would be cold up north. She packed as many of her winter clothes as possible.

She found her address book and took her bag back to Teri's place. If they decided to trace her phone calls, maybe they wouldn't think to check Teri's. With Teri's fertile imagination, Leslie was confident that Teri could explain away a call to Michigan.

Now Leslie looked at Jason and said, "I woke my cousin up. I apologized and asked him if I could use his cottage. He told me where to find the key and hung up. I doubt that he remembers the phone call.

"I was so careful to use cash so they couldn't trace me and yet, here they are, right on my trail and making up lies about why they're looking for me."

"They've got some good motivation going, honey. You've got the information that could put them behind bars for a long time. Were they in uniform when you saw them in the parking lot?"

"I don't think so, but they were wearing uniforms when I saw them approaching my apartment building "

He stood and limped away from her.

"You're putting weight on your leg," she said in surprise.

He poured himself more coffee, held the pot up in silent invitation and when she shook her head, placed it back on the burner. "I figure if I'm going to help you out of this mess, I need both legs."

"You must be in pain."

"I'm used to it. Besides, this is more important."

"There's no reason for you to get involved. This is too dangerous."

"What will you do if I don't? If they're looking for you along this road, they must have found out where your cousin's place is located."

"I realize that. I guess they can use the police network to find out all kinds of things."

His smile was dangerous. "So can I."

"Really? Are you connected with the police?"

"Nope. Even better. I have a contact who has the federal database at his disposal."

"Oh. Who?"

Jason picked up the phone as he answered. "My brother."

Six

Jason put in the call and listened as the phone rang. When the National Security Agency's operator answered, he said, "Jude Crenshaw, please."

"One moment."

He waited some more while he listened to all the clicking as the call was transferred. One thing about the NSA: they had the safest, most protected, phone system appropriations money could buy.

"Mr. Crenshaw's office," a male voice said.

"I'd like to speak to him, if I may."

"I'm sorry." and the man sounded sincere "—Mr. Crenshaw is in a meeting at the moment and asked that I hold all his calls."

"I understand. Will you ask him to call his brother—"

"Oh! I didn't realize…I have standing orders to put through any calls from family members, regardless of what he's doing. One moment, please."

Several minutes ticked by before Jason heard another click on the line.

"Hey, bro! It's always great to hear from you. Mind telling me which brother is calling?" Jude asked, chuckling.

"Jase. Look, I need—"

"Jase! Damn, but it's good to hear from you! How've you been? Are you in the States? Overseas? Or can you say?"

Jase sighed. Now he would face the consequences of not telling his family what had happened to him earlier, but there was nothing he could do about that now. Leslie needed some serious help and he knew he couldn't provide it for her.

"I'm in Michigan. Look, I—"

"Michigan! Who assigned you there? When I was in Delta, we worked strictly overseas."

"So do we. I'm on leave."

"In Michigan?" Jude sounded astonished.

"Look, I'll fill you in on all the details, but I need to explain why I'm calling."

"Shoot."

Jase quickly ran through the information Leslie had given him. When he finished Jase said, "They came looking for her this morning and I don't think these guys are going to let her get away from them. I need your help on several levels."

"You've got it."

"Can you do a search and find out everything you can about the local authorities in Deer Creek County, Tennessee? Find out what's going on if you can and if these two guys are mavericks or part of a bigger operation down there."

"Can do. Next?"

"I need to find Leslie a safe place to stay until this matter's resolved and those yahoos are put in jail."

Jude laughed. "Let me guess. She's single, she's beautiful and you're lusting after her."

"You're not too far off the mark there, bro, but that's besides the point. Do you know of a safe house where she—"

"Of course I do. And so do you."

"What do you mean?"

"Take her to the ranch."

Jason felt like he'd been knocked over the head with a mallet. He'd never thought of the ranch. But then, he hadn't intended to go with her. He just wanted to help her out of the bind she was in through no fault of her own.

He wasn't ready to go to ranch just yet. After all, he was settled in at the cabin; he had everything he needed and, most important, he had time to heal. Except now that Jude knew where he was, the whole family would know within hours.

His normal mode of communication was e-mails and he tried to stay current on what his family was doing. Since he'd never told them where he was, e-mail had worked just fine.

Until now.

Damn.

"Jase?" Jude asked. "You still there?"

"Uh, yeah. I guess I never thought about taking her somewhere, much less taking her home."

"Probably because you know you're going to catch hell for going to Michigan instead of Texas for your leave."

There was no help for him. He could insist on the

government taking care of her. He glanced over at her. She sat watching him, her eyes wide with fear. She had no one to depend on, except for her friend, Teri, and Leslie made it clear that she didn't want Teri to be involved any more than she already was.

On the other hand, if he went home now, he wouldn't be able to hide the fact that he'd been wounded.

"Jase?"

"Yeah."

"Don't tell me you're so scared to face the folks that you don't want to go home! What's really going on with you?"

So. Here it was. Confession time.

"I didn't want anyone to know until I was completely mobile that my squad was ambushed a few months ago. Those of us who survived were shot up pretty badly."

Jude didn't respond right away. When he did, his voice was very quiet. He sounded like Dad when he was angry. The angrier Dad got, the quieter he talked. "I see. And you didn't feel the need to share with the family that you were almost killed?"

"Well, if you put it that way—"

"What other way can you put it, Jason? How badly were you hurt?"

"Uh, took one in the leg, side and shoulder. I'm doing better, though."

"Oh, well, then that's all that matters, right? To hell with looking for support from your family, letting them care for you while you're recuperating. Do you ever think of anybody but yourself? Obviously not," Jude said in disgust.

This was every bit as bad as he'd expected. Worse, maybe. Jude had always been able to make him feel like crap. Maybe it was because they were closer in age than he was to his two older brothers. He'd always looked up to Jude, even when Jude got in so much trouble as a teenager…probably *because* he was always doing something he shouldn't have been doing.

Jase had joined the army, just like Jude, and when he had the chance, he became a part of Delta Force, just like Jude.

"You're right," Jase finally said. He couldn't hide the weariness in his voice.

"If you think that's going to make everything better, you might want to think again."

"I couldn't face them, especially you. I've been too ashamed."

"For what? Almost getting yourself killed?"

"For not saving the ones we lost."

"Ah. The Messiah complex. Don't know exactly how to break the news to you, bro, but you're far from god-like. So give it up."

Jase didn't say anything. He couldn't say anything. A knot had formed in his throat so big he could scarcely swallow. Was that what he'd done? Had he convinced himself that, despite everything that had happened, he should have saved them, no matter what?

"Jase? You still there?"

"Yeah."

"Talk to me."

Jase cleared his throat. "I'm feeling a little strange. Your butt kicking actually makes me feel better."

"Yeah, well, you should be used to it now. At least you're taking some interest in someone other than your-self. Tell me something about your friend—what did you say her name was?"

"Leslie O'Brien. She's an accountant and lives in Deer Creek, Tennessee."

"How old is she? What does she look like?"

"Jude, lay off, will you?"

"For now, maybe. So why don't you want to take her home to meet the family? You aren't ashamed of her, are you?"

"It's not like that, Jude." He glanced over at Leslie who was still focused on him. He kept his eyes on her and said, "She showed up here in the middle of a snow-storm day before yesterday. We barely know each other."

When he caught her eye, he grinned and winked at her. He loved to see her blush, which was what she was doing right now.

"Whatever," Jude was saying. "Do you remember the names of the two cops who showed up?"

Jason told him. Jude repeated them as he was no doubt writing them down. "Do they know who you are?"

"No. If they check the deed records, they still won't know because I'm staying in an army buddy's cabin."

"That's going to make it much easier to lose them. Do you think you convinced them you didn't know her?"

"Maybe. Since her car slid off into a ditch and the snowplows had already been through before they arrived, I doubt they could see it."

"Will they recognize it if they do see it?"

"I don't know. I'm not sure how they managed to trace her this far. Regardless of what else they are, they're damn good investigators."

"They have lots of motivation behind them. You got wheels?"

"I bought an old Jeep. Why?"

"You need to get to Texas without alerting any authorities."

"I don't know, Jude. I'm not sure I can handle driving that many miles right now."

Silence. Then, "Oh, little brother, what aren't you telling me? Can you walk?"

"I'm using a cane, but I was hit on my right side, which is the leg I need—"

"To drive with. Gotcha." After a moment Jude said, "Let Leslie drive."

Once again Jase glanced at her. She was staring off into space now, as though she were many miles away. "That would work," he finally said, wondering what she was thinking.

"Then here's what you do. Get to a car dealer, somewhere, somehow, and buy yourself a car that can make it to Texas. You can leave the car at the ranch once your leave is over."

"I could do that, I suppose."

"Can you call a taxi to get into town?"

"Better than that, I can get a tow truck out here and rescue her car." He continued to watch Leslie. "I kind of like the idea of having a good-looking woman as a chauffeur." That got her attention. She stared at him in surprise.

"Fine. Get out of there as soon as you can. I'll alert the parents you're heading home."

"Thanks, Jude," he said gruffly, touched by the offer to run interference for him. "I appreciate it."

"Of course, that doesn't let you off the hook. You might as well face the fact that you're going to catch hell from everyone."

Jase smiled, feeling like a hundred-pound weight

had been lifted off his shoulders. "With you running interference for me, I'll be fine."

Jude laughed. "Just like in high school." He paused and then said, "Oh, by the way, have you heard that I just became a father last week?"

"No kidding! Well, congratulations, Daddy. Is it a boy or a girl?"

"Actually, it's two boys. Carina and I had twins."

Jase burst into laughter. "Well, I'd love to see you up feeding twins at two o'clock in the morning."

"Give me some time. I'm getting the hang of it."

"I'll let you go. Sorry about pulling you out of your meeting."

"I'm not. I was fighting not to fall asleep. Some people are so enamored of their own voice they get carried away. Stay in touch, now, okay? I mean it. I need to know where you are every step of the way, especially if you spot those goons. I'll find out if anything is going on in that county. If there's isn't, I'll make damn sure something gets started!"

"Thanks, Jude. For everything. Guess I needed to have my butt kicked."

"Any time, bro. Any time."

Jase hung up and stood staring at the phone, going over their conversation.

"You and your brother are really close, aren't you?" Leslie said, pulling him out of his reverie.

He moved to the large recliner and carefully lowered himself. "Yeah."

"Did he have a baby recently?"

"Two. Twin boys. I forgot to ask him what they named them."

"So what does he suggest I do?"

"He suggested that we—" he emphasized the word "—go to Texas as soon as I can get us some transportation."

She looked startled. "Why Texas?"

"Because that's where I live when I'm not on duty."

"I don't understand. Why does he expect you to stay with me?"

"It's probably his way of making sure I go see the family."

"I hate to be the one causing you to leave here."

He shrugged. "Can't be helped. As soon as I told him I was Stateside and wasn't home, I was busted, big time. I need to go home before they start imagining all kinds of things that might have happened to me. Actually, it will work out just fine. I can let you drive, if you don't mind, and I'll finish recuperating at home."

"But I don't know your family."

"You didn't know me, either, but somehow we're planning a trip together."

She frowned. "I suppose you're right." She paused. "I heard you say you weren't up to driving. We can take my car."

"Not a good idea to take your car. My guess is that they discovered where your cousin lived and headed north. No doubt they've already talked to the man who rented you the car and could have a stolen vehicle watch out for it."

"Oh, no!" she said, aghast.

"I think we should play it safe. We'll get the rental into town and I'll pay someone to drive it back to Deer Creek. If he's stopped for any reason, I'll have him refer them to Jude in D.C. They may decide not to follow up on it. Do you have any idea what the rate is?"

She told him and he nodded. "I'll make certain that

the garage is paid as well as the driver. And maybe it would be a good idea to have Jude call your neighbor to see if she's been hassled by those two. Can you think of anything you might have Jude say that will convince her the call is for you and not a trick to find you?"

She thought for several moments. "Well, she has a pet iguana named Sam. Not too many people actually know that because we aren't supposed to have pets of any kind in the apartments."

"Okay. I'll call Jude at home this evening. We've got lots to do before dark."

"I feel awful getting you involved in all of this."

"That's the breaks. Like it or not, I *am* involved. I can't think of any other way to keep you safe than to take you to a part of the country where they would never think to look for you."

"Won't your parents mind?"

"Not in the least. They're nothing like me. They're super-nice people."

"You're nice."

"You didn't think so when you first got here."

"True. But I figured you must be in a lot of pain and didn't like the idea of dealing with another person."

"I guess I got used to the idea."

"Well," she said with a sigh. "My options are extremely limited at the moment. Thank you for being willing to take me to your home."

"You're welcome. Now that we have that settled, I'll call a wrecker to come get your car and offer a bonus to do it by one o'clock. We'll ride in with the driver and I'll buy a car for us to use."

She looked at him in wonder. "Just like that? You'll buy a car?"

He smiled. "The thing is, all the Crenshaws receive a steady income from the various businesses the family owns. I've been banking mine because I didn't need it. I think I'll have enough to get a car," he said with a grin.

He grabbed the phone book and looked for a tow truck company in the Yellow Pages.

Several hours later they stood in the showroom of one of the high-end car dealerships. Leslie felt like Alice had when she fell down the rabbit hole. None of this seemed real.

She watched Jason discuss with the sales manager of the car dealership the kind of car he wanted. Once the manager discovered that Jason intended to pay cash—he had his bank standing by to wire the money directly to the dealership—things moved at lightning speed.

Leslie wasn't particularly surprised to see that Jason settled on a sports car. Within an hour they drove the car out of the showroom and left for the cabin with Leslie driving.

"You buy a car as casually as I buy a pair of shoes on sale," she finally said into the silence that had fallen between them.

"Hmm," he said absently. "Do you think you can get this thing up to the cabin without getting stuck?"

She glanced at him from the corner of her eye. "Probably not."

"That's what I'm afraid of." He pulled a cell phone from his pocket and hit a number. When the phone was answered, he said, "Hey, Kevin, I know this is really short notice and all, but I need my driveway cleared out as soon as possible. I'll double your payment if you could come now." A pause. "Sounds good, man. I'm coming from town. You'll probably beat me there."

When they approached the cabin turnoff Leslie saw a young man seated on a tractor with a snow blade attached to the front. The graveled driveway was cleared of most of the snow.

Jase hit the button to lower his window as Kevin got off the tractor and ambled over to where they'd stopped.

"Nice wheels, Jason. Really nice."

"Thanks."

"Had her long?"

"Not too long." He pulled his wallet from his pocket. "Thanks for your trouble, Kevin. I really appreciate your help."

"Any time," the teenager said with a wave before he returned to the tractor. They waited until Kevin pulled onto the road on his way home and then Leslie turned the car into the driveway leading to the cabin.

She stopped in front of the porch. "It won't take me long to get my things together, how about you?"

Jason eased the door open and got out. "Same here. We may have to empty the pantry and bring it along."

"I can do that. You can also show me what you need packed."

They had reached the top of the porch by then and Jason unlocked the door. "You don't have to coddle me, Leslie. I'm used to looking after myself."

She followed him inside and closed the door. "A little touchy, aren't you? I thought you wanted to get out of here tonight. I'm offering to speed things up."

Jason had the grace to look embarrassed. "Sorry. I keep most of my stuff in my locker so there's little to do there. I'll feel much better when we get away from here."

Leslie looked around the cabin with a certain amount of fondness. "I'm surprised to realize that I've enjoyed being here."

Jason stood over his locker and folded some of the items inside, making room for the rest of his things. He glanced up. She wondered what he was thinking. Finally he grinned and replied, "That could be because of the company you keep."

She threw a stray sock at him and he laughed.

She already felt safer, knowing that Jason would be with her.

Seven

"Maybe you should have gotten a larger car."

Leslie stood nearby, watching Jason put their belongings in the trunk. Without turning around, he said, "It will all fit. Just needs to be packed right."

After a couple of minutes he straightened and said, "There. I told you. There's a lot more room in the trunk than you'd think, considering the size of the car." He turned and picked up the cane that was propped against the back fender. "I think that's it." He looked at his watch. "It's almost eight o'clock. Let's get going."

"I'm glad we're leaving under the cover of darkness."

He nodded. "I'll lock the cabin, then, and you can warm up the car."

Leslie was more than willing to get out of the cold. The sky was clear tonight and the temperature had dropped. She hurriedly got into the car and started the engine.

She'd never driven anything as powerful as Jason's new sports car and she was nervous behind the wheel. She'd taken her time driving back to the cabin, learning where everything was located. She listened to the soft rumble of the engine, which almost sounded like the purr of a big jungle cat.

Jason opened the passenger's door and sat down. "That's it. Let's go."

Once they reached the interstate, Jason glanced at his watch and pulled out his cell phone. He pushed a couple of buttons and waited. When someone answered, he said, "Hey, it's me. We're on the interstate and heading south." After a moment he said, "We'll go until Leslie gets tired of driving. Did you find out anything about that Tennessee county?"

Leslie wished she could hear what Jason's brother was saying because Jason had stopped talking, except for an occasional question. When he finally spoke again, all he said was, "Sounds good. I'll call you in the morning," and hung up.

"What did he find out?"

Jason stretched his back before settling into the seat. "You live in a wide-open county, Ms. O'Brien. I'm surprised you didn't know that."

She glanced at him before immediately refocusing on the highway in front of them. "I don't know what a wide-open county is."

"Where the law looks the other way while there's gambling and prostitution and unsavory types collect money from the business owners for—" he held two fingers up, wriggling them "—protection."

"You mean, like gangsters."

"Yes, ma'am. That's exactly what I mean. The FBI

has someone undercover down there because of the number of complaints from others who live there."

"I had no idea. Do they know who that man was that I saw shot?"

"One of the mayor's aides has turned up missing. Word is that he embezzled money from the city's coffers and took off. Funny thing, though. Nobody shows any interest in looking for him. His wife refuses to believe it and so do the feds."

"It gets worse and worse, doesn't it?"

"Yes and no. When Jude told the agents that there was a witness who saw a man murdered, they were glad to hear that you'd managed to get out of town safely. Right now they're working to find out who's running the operations. Is it the sheriff, or has the department been sufficiently bribed by someone else to look the other way? Because of what you saw, the agents are considering the theory that the deputies have another job on the side. You can't help them with that. They just want you to be somewhere safe, which Jude assured them you would be."

"Did he reach Teri?"

"Not yet. He's going to keep trying until he gets her. If she's in any danger he'll let the Bureau know and get protection for her."

"That makes me feel a little better. But until I actually know she's okay I can't help but worry."

They rode along in silence after that. Leslie paid no attention to the time because all that mattered to her was getting out of Michigan as soon as possible.

The Welcome To Indiana greeting flashed by some hours later and Jason spoke for the first time in a couple of hours.

"There's a Holiday Inn billboard. Why don't we stop there for the night?"

"Sounds good to me."

Leslie began to watch for the exit number that had been on the sign. She was exhausted, not just physically, but mentally and emotionally, as well.

She'd spent her driving time reviewing all that had happened to her since she'd left home, wondering if there was something she could have done differently. Here she was traveling with a man she barely knew and would soon be staying with people she didn't know at all. She'd thought about contacting her cousin so that some family member would know where she was, but she didn't dare in case the deputies were monitoring his phone.

Leslie knew this trip was hard for Jason in more ways than one. He certainly didn't act as though he was counting the hours before reaching his family.

She looked forward to having a room to herself for some much needed privacy tonight. From the grim look on Jason's face, he must be in a great deal of pain. He was probably as eager as she was to have some alone time.

Once on the access road, Leslie followed the signs until she turned into the hotel driveway.

"You'd better stay here in the car," he said once they'd stopped in front of the lobby. "The fewer people who see you while we're traveling, the better." He paused and looked at her. "By the way, where did they get a photo of you?"

"I have no idea, unless it was from my driver's license."

He nodded. "Probably was. Frankly, I don't think anybody's going to recognize you from that photo."

She grinned. "I suppose that's a good thing."

"Oh, yeah. You're much better looking than the

photo. I'll be back in a minute." He eased out of the car, picked up his cane and slowly walked inside the lobby.

She was a little dazed by his remark. Neither one of them had brought up the kiss they'd shared, was it just this morning? He'd probably thought nothing of it. She'd been available; he'd kissed her. No big deal as far as he was concerned.

It was a big deal to her because the kiss had stirred her in ways she'd never experienced and her reaction bothered her. Jason was very handsome and, when he chose to be, he was extremely charming. With everything else that was going on, Leslie felt vulnerable in ways she'd never thought about until now.

Being so close to him in the car didn't help matters. The subtle aroma of his aftershave mingled with the purely masculine scent of a healthy male was a heady combination.

Leslie could see him at the registration counter. In his sheepskin-lined coat and wearing close-fitting jeans, he looked rugged and capable of taking on anyone who gave him trouble, even using a cane. Despite the lateness of the hour, there were people in the lobby returning to their rooms or waiting to check in. She noticed that each woman had watched him as he'd approached the registration desk.

There should be a law against looking so irresistible.

She watched the desk clerk hand him an envelope and show him on a map where to find their rooms. Jason nodded and walked away.

His limp was very pronounced now and she knew he must be in terrible pain to give in to it like that. She hoped he'd take some of his pain medication so that he could rest tonight.

Once inside the car Jason said, "We didn't talk about this, but I decided that we need to stay in the same room. For one thing, if anyone's looking for you, they won't be expecting you to be a part of a couple, which is a plus. I'd sleep better knowing you were nearby."

So much for a little alone time. She started the car. Without looking at him she said, "All right."

After a pause he asked, "You aren't going to argue?"

"I'm too tired to argue. I just want to find a bed. As far as that goes, we've spent the past two nights in the same room. This isn't all that different."

"Good point." He nodded his head and said, "Drive around to the side of the building. We're on the lower floor. The clerk probably figured I didn't need a set of stairs to climb."

When they got out of the car, she said, "We don't want to drag our luggage in there, do we?"

Jason shook his head. "No. Let's get what we need for tonight and in the morning."

Leslie wearily pawed through her clothes, grabbed her bag of toiletries, her pajamas, what she intended to wear tomorrow and closed the bag. She waited while Jason got his things and then she closed and locked the car. He led the way to the room, unlocked the door and ushered her inside.

Jason flipped on the light switch, revealing a room with two double beds and a large bathroom to the side. "All the comforts of home," he murmured, closing and locking the door behind them. "Go ahead and shower. I can wait."

Leslie didn't need to hear his offer twice. She stepped inside the bathroom and shut the door. Soon she stood under the welcoming warmth of the shower and closed her eyes.

All she wanted to do was to get horizontal.

She was already in bed asleep before Jason went into the bathroom for his shower.

Jason woke up and glanced at the clock beside his bed. It was almost ten o'clock. Of course they hadn't stopped until almost one last night. Time really didn't matter since they weren't in any great hurry. At least, he wasn't. To say that he wasn't looking forward to his homecoming was a vast understatement.

As much as he loved his family, he dreaded facing them and explaining his need to be alone to adjust to everything that had happened. He still wasn't sure how his plans had blown up in his face.

Of course he did. She was sound asleep in the other bed.

On the positive side, he supposed that having Leslie with him would be a buffer between him and those who loved him. At least for a few hours.

He'd take whatever he could get.

He rolled over and faced her bed. She had her back to him and all he could see were some small curls peeking out of the covers where her head must be.

Jude had been right. He was lusting for her, which had been quite a surprise since his body hadn't stirred at the sight of a woman in a long time. At first he thought his reaction was because he'd been alone for so long. Now he wasn't so sure. There was something about Leslie that got to him.

He wasn't certain what it was that specifically drew him to her. Maybe it was no more than the damsel-in-distress syndrome that had brought them together, but somehow he didn't think so. He liked her. She stood up for herself and yet appeared almost shy at times.

He wished he'd met her mother. The woman must have been very wise to bring up such a lovely daughter. A lovely, innocent, daughter.

It was that innocence that made him a little nervous. All right, a lot nervous. She didn't have to tell him that she wasn't the type to jump into bed with a guy for a breezy, no-strings-attached affair.

And that was the only kind he'd ever had…or wanted. Wasn't it?

She stirred and turned over. When she saw that he was awake, she smiled and said, "Good morning."

"Yeah," he said gruffly, disturbed by his thoughts. "I guess we need to get moving. I thought we'd go have breakfast at the restaurant across the street and keep moving south."

She nodded. "Okay." She reached for her housecoat at the bottom of the bed and put it on as she pushed the covers away. "I feel so much better this morning. I don't think I moved all night."

Jason wished he could say the same. His thigh muscles had protested every time he'd moved last night.

"I won't be more than a few minutes," she said, gathering her things and going into the bathroom. As soon as the door closed, he got up and dressed, then went to the window and opened the dark drapes.

The sky was gray with plump clouds making pyramids in the sky. They'd probably get more snow today. He thought about Leslie driving in snow and smiled. He might offer to start out the day at the wheel. When he got tired, she could take over and perhaps by then, they would be south enough so that any moisture would be rain.

Surely she knew how to drive in rain.

He called Jude and this time was put straight through.

"Just thought I'd let you know we're in northern Indiana this morning and heading to St. Louis."

"I got a description of the missing man. They told me he's about five-eight, maybe a hundred fifty pounds, reddish hair—"

"That's our guy, I could bet on it." Leslie came into the room and sat at the end of her bed, watching his face. "Hold on, Jude," he said, and repeated the description to her. She nodded.

"Yeah, she couldn't see his features, but general build and his hair showed up in the parking lot light."

"So you two getting along all right?"

"Sure. Why not?"

"Just checking. I'm going to get in touch with her friend and I'll call back when I find out anything."

"Almost forgot. When you reach her, there's a code so that she'll know you aren't one of the bad guys."

"Okay."

"Mention Sam."

"Sam?"

"Teri's pet iguana. That way she'll know for sure you've spoken to Leslie."

Jude laughed. "Sam, the iguana, huh? All right."

"Have you talked to the folks yet?"

"Here's what I did, Jase. I called Jake last night and we had an hour-long discussion about your situation. He said he'd go over to see the folks this morning and talk to them. He knows they're going to be devastated that they hadn't heard you were hurt. He wants to talk them through it. I explained to him what it's like being out there on those missions and being responsible for others. I told him I could understand your reaction. I didn't agree with it, but I understood it."

"All right."

"He plans for you and Leslie to stay there at the main ranch house. Any stranger coming onto the property will be closely checked out."

"Even if they're law enforcement?"

"Especially if they're law enforcement. He intends to alert the sheriff in New Eden, as well, in case he gets any police bulletins about her."

"Good. I have to say that those two are good with their stories. They almost had me convinced she was an escaped felon."

"The sheriff won't be fooled, believe me."

"Good."

"I'll get back to you," Jude said, and they hung up.

Jason looked at Leslie. "Everything's fine. You don't have anything to worry about."

"How long will I have to stay?"

He shrugged. "Can't tell you. We'll have to see how all of this develops. Right now they need to find the man that you saw or his body."

"I'll have to testify, won't I?"

"Too soon to say. Let's just take it a day at a time, okay?"

She nodded.

"So let's go eat. I'm starving." He didn't intend for Leslie to know the amount of pain he was dealing with this morning. He'd overdone it yesterday. Maybe he wouldn't mention driving unless it began to snow.

By the time they finished eating, rain thundered down from the skies. "Would you prefer that I drive?" Jason asked.

"Won't that be too much for your leg?"

"Well, I'll see how it goes. If it's too much, I'll let you take over. Believe me, I'm no martyr."

Leslie insisted on getting the car and bringing it to the entrance of the restaurant. By the time they switched seats so that he could drive, his phone rang. Before he answered it, Jason said, "Maybe I can coax you into massaging my leg for me when we stop for the night."

"I think that can be arranged."

He took the call.

"Hi, this is Jude. Is Leslie nearby?"

"She's sitting here in the car next to me. Why?"

"I've patched through a call for her so she can talk to her very suspicious friend who refuses to believe I'm in touch with Leslie."

"Okay." He handed the phone to Leslie. "Teri wants to speak to you."

She looked shocked and grabbed his phone. "Teri? Is that you?"

Jude answered. "Hold on and I'll switch the call."

A moment later Leslie heard Teri say, "Hello? Who is this?"

Leslie laughed in delight. "Teri! Hi! It's me."

"Leslie? Oh, thank God. I've been worried sick about you. Who's the guy who called talking about Sam? Was that your cousin? Are you okay?"

"I'm okay, thanks to a soldier who's helping me."

"A soldier? Didn't know you fraternized with any."

"First time for everything. You see, I ran into a snowstorm about thirty miles from my cousin's place and ended up getting stuck. Jason Crenshaw, the soldier I mentioned, gave me a place to stay during the storm. How are you?"

"Oh, we're doing fine here. I've just been really worried, wondering if you made it okay. Sounds like you had a little trouble."

"Not only the storm. Those two guys found out I was in Michigan and came looking for me."

"Oh, that's horrible. After everything we did to get you away from them."

"Jason told them he hadn't seen me. But, Teri! You aren't going to believe this. They told him I was an escaped felon! Can you believe it?"

"They're desperate. What can I say? So you're staying with this soldier?"

"Jason. That's right. He has a brother, Jude, who works for the government. He's the one who set up this call. I thought mentioning Sam might let you know that I was all right."

"I wasn't taking any chances. What do you intend to do now?"

"Jason is taking me to his family in Texas until it's safe for me to come home."

"Oh. So Jason's married. How old is he, by the way?"

Leslie glanced at Jason. "Nope, not married. Thirty."

Jason lifted an eyebrow quizzically.

"But you said his family…"

"Another brother and his wife. Oh! Jason hired someone to take Ed's car back to him. Thank goodness the car wasn't damaged. You might want to tell Ed to be looking for him. Have those men contacted you again?"

Teri chuckled. "Once. I guess that was enough. When they knocked, Charlie answered the door."

"The old intimidator, himself, huh? That's priceless. Too bad they don't know he's a teddy bear."

"Shh. That's our secret. Anyway, he told them he

knew nothing about you or where you might be in a tone that said he didn't want them harassing us. I think they got the message."

"I guess so. He could pick both of them up, one in each hand, and not break a sweat."

"Yep. That's my little darlin', all right."

"I would have loved to see the looks on their faces."

"Is there a way I can reach you?"

"I'll get back with you on that, but there is one more thing you can do. Would you call my boss and explain that I was called away suddenly on a family emergency—which certainly isn't a lie!—and that I'll be back as soon as possible?"

"No problem. Anything else?"

"Maybe clean out my refrigerator and water my plants?"

"I'll move the plants over here for the duration. I'll hang on to your mail, unless you want me to forward it."

"I'll have to find out about that, as well. I really appreciate all you've done for me."

"It scares me to think about what you would have done if I hadn't been here. I came this close to going with Charlie on his trip last week."

"My guardian angel must be looking out for me."

"Somebody is. And, uh, let me know more about this Jason guy when you can talk freely."

"Not much more to tell, but sure. I'll be in touch."

She handed the phone back to Jason.

He hung up and looked at her. "She okay?"

"Yes, thank goodness." She looked out the car window. "It's stopped raining. Let me drive so you don't do anything to your leg."

He thought about it for a moment and then nodded.

"I'll take you up on that. I'll make a deal with you. I'll drive until we stop for lunch."

She looked at him in wonder. He'd put his life on hold to help her. She owed him so much. "I couldn't have done this without you. You have my undying gratitude."

"Good. My reward will be the massage I'll get tonight."

Eight

"We're approaching St. Louis," Jason said about six that night. "I know it's a little early but I'd like to find a hotel there." He'd been driving in rain for several hours.

Leslie stirred from a doze. "You're hurting, aren't you? I told you I could drive longer."

He glanced at her with a smile. "I'll come clean. I wanted to see how the car handled. I'm pleased to say that I really like this thing."

She stretched and yawned. "I know. I'm already spoiled. My car is at least eight years old."

Jason drove through St. Louis until he reached the southwest outskirts and pulled into another well-known hotel chain. This time he had their luggage taken up to their room.

"Do you want to grab something to eat before we go up?" he asked Leslie once he'd registered. "Then we won't have to go out in this weather anymore for the evening."

"Sounds good," she said, "unless you don't want me to be seen by too many people."

He eased back into the car and pulled away from the hotel. "We can take care of both. I know this great little Italian restaurant that I think you'll like. I hope you like Italian?"

"I'm easy to please."

Once inside the restaurant Leslie realized what Jason meant. The booths were high and private and the lighting was low, each table holding a large squat candle.

Once they ordered, she looked around. "When you said little, you meant it literally, didn't you?"

"One of my army buddies is from St. Louis and we've been here on leave a couple of times. It's very low-key and has fantastic food."

She fidgeted with her napkin. "When do you think we'll get to the ranch?"

"If we get a decent start in the morning, I figure we can get to Dallas tomorrow night, although it may be late. We'll get a good night's sleep and drive to the ranch, which is about four hours or so from Dallas."

"I feel so strange, going home with you. I don't want to give anyone the wrong idea about me."

"Don't worry. Jude's told them what happened to you and, knowing my dad and my oldest brother, Jake, who runs the ranch now, they'd insist you stay there whether or not I was along."

"But no one seems to know how long I'll need to stay. Hopefully, I still have a job to go back to."

They were both tired and hungry and fell silent once the food arrived. Leslie savored each bite. The truth was that she'd seen more of the country in the past week than she'd ever seen. She and her mom hadn't traveled much. Instead, they were avid readers, or as her mom would say, they were armchair travelers.

Seeing the huge arch as they neared St. Louis had been a thrill and she acknowledged that she'd missed more than she'd thought by staying home all these years.

What she didn't particularly enjoy was the rain that had dogged them most of the day. She'd been relieved when Jason had taken over driving. He'd kept saying he was okay all the while the grooves around his mouth deepened as the afternoon wore on.

"Jason?" Leslie said while they had dessert and coffee.

He looked inquiringly at her.

"Why are you doing this?"

"Doing what?"

"Going to the trouble of taking me to your family home. You seemed settled at your cabin alone. You were far from pleased when I showed up. What changed?"

He took his time answering. "You're right. I went to the cabin because I didn't want to be around anyone. I needed time to come to grips with my life. Call it an early midlife crisis. Neither one of us had a realistic choice when you showed up at my door but for you to stay." He reached for his glass of water. After drinking, he continued. "I think that it helped me to focus on something—and someone—else for a while, even though I'll admit I resented your disturbing my winter lair. I suppose what changed was the knowledge that you were running from a situation over which you had no control. You were scared—for good reason—and the fact that you were traced to Michigan gave me some idea of what you were up against." He smiled a little.

"I'd packed away my savior suit and had no intention of jumping into a situation that had nothing to do with me…until I couldn't ignore the injustice of what was happening to you."

"I see."

"Of course, Jude might have been right when he suggested that I was attracted to you."

"He said that?"

"In so many words, yes. I can't discount the fact that I find you intriguing."

"Me? There's nothing intriguing about me. I'm so ordinary even my dentist doesn't recognize me when I show up for my yearly checkup!"

"In that case, your dentist must be in his eighties and very forgetful."

"Well, as to that. He *is* talking about retiring."

"It's hard to explain. You have a freshness about you, a willingness to do your best to deal with whatever comes at you. You managed to get away from those apes, giving yourself a few days' lead." He grinned suddenly, his bright smile flashing. "And I find you very attractive."

"Oh." What could she say to that?

"For instance, I've been enjoying the way the candlelight is reflected in your eyes, causing them to glow like amber. I have trouble keeping myself from watching your mouth because it has a sensuousness that contradicts the innocence in your eyes."

She wanted to slide under the table in embarrassment. She felt as if he were whispering these things in her ear. Leslie straightened instead and even though she knew her face was flaming she refused to follow the impulse of covering her face with her hands. "Are you trying to seduce me?" She didn't sound as stern as she'd hoped. In fact, she sounded more than a little breathless.

He placed his hand over hers. "I don't know," he murmured. "Is it working?"

"I know you're having a little fun but I don't know how to play your game."

He frowned. "There's no game, Leslie, unless it's the eternal pull between man and woman, male and female, that has always been a part of the species."

She slipped her hand from his. "I'm not looking for a casual relationship with someone."

"What are you looking for?"

Her mind drifted back to her childhood. "I'd like to find someone who I could love and who would love me. I know that my mother idealized the relationship she had with my father. They'd been married less than two years when he was killed and yet I grew up with stories of their relationship and I was touched by their devotion. When I grew older she let me read the letters he wrote to her so that I could get some idea of the kind of man my father was. I know I sound hopelessly naive about relationships, but you asked."

"Actually, I'm impressed that you know what you want. Your mother may have idealized their relationship but I saw one just like that first-hand when I was growing up."

"Your parents?"

He nodded. "When I grew older I realized how fortunate I'd been to have witnessed the deep love and respect they have for each other. I thought all relationships were that way until I moved out into the world. So I agree with you, that's a healthy goal to have." He glanced at his watch. "Are you ready to go?"

She nodded, unable to find her voice at the moment.

"If we're going to get an early start, we need to get some rest."

Leslie thought about what Jason had said to her during their drive back to the hotel. Once in their room they followed the same routine as the night before. Jason was leaning heavily on his cane when he came out of the bathroom.

She shook her head. "I've never known anyone as stubborn as you!" she exclaimed, throwing the covers back and getting out of bed.

He eased down onto his bed. "I'll be okay. The muscles in my leg keep going into spasms."

"Lie down and I'll massage it for you, help you to relax."

He made a face. "I was joking about that massage, you know. Take my word for it, there's no way I'm going to relax with your hands on me."

"Would a pain pill help?"

"No doubt. But I need my wits about me."

She placed her hands on her hips. "Either take something for the pain or let me help you."

He stretched out on the bed and closed his eyes. "You win," he said wearily.

Leslie had done her best to ignore the fact that the only thing Jason had on was a towel around his waist. The scar on his shoulder stood in sharp relief against his tanned skin.

"Could you, uh, would you mind turning over?" she finally asked.

He turned without saying anything and buried his head beneath his pillow.

All right. She could do this. She found some body lotion in her toiletry bag and poured it on her hands.

When she placed her hands on his shoulders and started working her fingers and thumbs into the rock-hard surface, he made a grunting sound.

He sounded muffled when he said, "That's not my leg."

She smiled, settling in more comfortably beside him. "I'm aware of that. However, you're so tied up in knots you're like a bowstring. Just relax and let me loosen some of these muscles."

"Where in the world did you learn how to do that?" he asked a little later, groaning with what she hoped was pleasure.

"A friend of mine was a massage therapist. She taught me."

"If I'd had any idea your fingers were so talented, I wouldn't have resisted your suggestion quite so strenuously."

She could feel the muscles along his spine slowly let go. He began to take deeper and longer breaths until he seemed to sink into the bed. When she discovered that he wore briefs beneath the towel, she moved it aside and worked on his backside and gingerly moved down to his thigh.

She winced at the scarring. The bullet had entered at an angle in his upper thigh and lodged near his knee. No wonder those muscles and tendons protested every time he used his leg.

Like the scars on his shoulder, those on his legs were nicely healed.

Leslie was working on his calves when he rolled over. She glanced at him, expecting to find him asleep. Instead his blue eyes glittered hotly. He whispered, "Come here," and Leslie leaned toward him, feeling as though she had no will of her own.

This kiss was nothing like the one they'd shared a couple of mornings ago. This one was searingly passionate, making her toes curl. She shifted and stretched out beside him. Jason pulled her on top of him, his arms wrapped firmly around her, no doubt taking her move as encouragement—and she knew it was.

Leslie lost herself in sensation until she realized that he was strongly aroused. She didn't want to tease him, but she couldn't continue like this. She eased away from him.

"I'm too heavy," she said, and slipped to his side.

He turned with her. "I love the way you kiss," he murmured. "Your mouth promises so much." He kissed her again.

She fought not to forget that she didn't want to let this go any further. Unfortunately her body wasn't listening.

Leslie stroked his chest, amazed at its width as well as the strong muscles along his neck and shoulders.

She stiffened when he slid his hand beneath her pajama top and ran his fingers up and down her spine. She arched her back and sighed.

He moved his hand until he cupped her small breast. She jerked away. "Please," she said, trying to catch her breath. "I can't—"

"I know," he said soothingly. "I promise I won't take advantage of you in any way. Just let me love you."

She trembled when he lifted her top and placed his mouth over one of her breasts. His gentleness was her undoing. Her breasts were so sensitive and his tongue caused the tips to harden. He pulled the nipple into his mouth and gave a gentle tug and she hugged his head to her.

Leslie had never been so aroused in her life. She could hardly breathe and she whimpered her need.

As though he knew how she felt, he slid his hand beneath her pajama bottoms and cupped the moist curls there. She pushed into his hand, almost sobbing.

He rubbed her there, allowing his finger entrance into the slickness and she strained her hips harder against him. With his thumb he continued to encircle the small nub that released a stream of sensation. She let out a soft cry and pulsated against him, on and on until she was limp.

He continued to stroke her, gradually moving his hand until it rested on her breast once more.

When she opened her eyes, she saw him watching her, his face taut.

"Jason, I—" She couldn't think of anything to say. She felt like she'd been caught in some kind of giant undertow where she'd lost all sense of direction until she'd been tossed limply onto the shore.

His touch was soothing now, his hands stroking her back.

She tried again. "I want to—" She touched him through his briefs. "You need to—" Once again words failed her.

He pressed her hand against his erection. "You don't have to do anything you don't want to."

She moved her hand until it disappeared beneath his briefs. "I want to," she whispered.

When he cried out in release sometime later, Leslie felt wonderfully rewarded. She gave him a lingering kiss and sat up.

He opened his eyes, looking more relaxed than she'd ever seen him. "Thank you."

She felt her checks flame. "It was, uh, the least I could do, under the circumstances. I hope you'll be able to sleep."

"I'd sleep much better if you slept here with me. At least now we have a double bed."

She knew that she was way over her head emotionally where Jason was concerned. How could she have possibly fallen so hard for someone she'd known only a few days?

Nine

Jason woke up early, fully awake and aware that Leslie was asleep on his uninjured shoulder, one arm and leg resting on top of him.

What did he think he was doing, anyway? Playing house?

The fact was that he'd slept better last night than he had in months. Having Leslie asleep in his arms felt natural and right, and the recognition scared him.

He eased his arm from beneath her. She stirred a moment before snuggling into her pillow. He slipped out of bed and went in to take a shower in the hope of getting his head on straight before he had to face her this morning.

While he stood under the stinging shower, Jason thought about what had happened the night before. When had the evening gotten so out of control? Her touch had erased all the reasons why he needed to keep their relationship casual. And yet…her hands moving along his body, their warmth and comfort, had eased aches he hadn't realized he had until they were gone.

Or had he lapsed into convenient amnesia when he'd rolled over and looked at her? She'd scrubbed her face and the lamp by the bed had given her a delicate glow. He smiled at the memory of her in her demure pajamas. Leslie didn't need seductive clothing to look sexy. How could he possibly have ignored the look in her eyes, a yearning she made no effort to hide?

The problem was what to do about this new intimacy between them. He had no business getting involved with her or with anyone until he got his life into some kind of order.

He'd wasted too much time wishing he could have saved the men in his squad; too much time brooding alone while his wounds healed. If it weren't for Leslie, he would still be there in the cabin, convinced he was where he needed—and wanted—to be.

His discussions with Jude completed what her sudden appearance in his life had started: he was taking a strong look at himself instead of wallowing in his painful and irreversible memories.

He didn't like what he saw.

In another couple of days he'd be seeing his family for the first time in two years. He hadn't made it back for Jude's wedding and had never met his wife, Carina. Jake had a son who would be two in a few months, and he'd never seen the boy.

Not that he'd had much control as to when he could take a leave…until a few months ago. So what had he done? Isolated himself and licked his wounds like some injured animal.

He finished rinsing himself and shut off the water. When he was dried and shaved, he realized that he'd have to wear a towel into the other room to get his clothes.

Considering what happened the night before, Leslie would probably think he intended to crawl back into bed with her, which wasn't going to happen. It irritated him that the thought had crossed his mind.

He just needed to hold on to his self-control until they reached the ranch and they would no longer be alone. A little self-discipline was all that he needed.

Unfortunately his stern admonishments flew out of his head when he walked into the bedroom and found Leslie standing with her back to him wearing nothing but her panties as she fastened her bra.

"Oops, sorry," he said, stopping in his tracks.

She whirled around and grabbed her robe, holding it in front of her. She wouldn't meet his eyes. The move would have been sufficient to cover her if she hadn't been standing in front of the mirror. He had a view of her lithe body and the way her waist narrowed only to curve into her enticing derriere.

"I thought I'd be dressed by the time you came out," she said faintly.

"I'll just grab some clothes and I'll be out of your way," he replied. Once he found what he planned to wear, he returned to the bathroom without looking at her again.

"Great, pal," he muttered to himself. "Thanks to your behavior last night, you've managed to destroy the easy relationship you had with her."

After he dressed, Jason opened the door. "You decent?" he asked.

"Yes."

Her answer sounded subdued. He walked into the bedroom and found that she wore dark brown slacks and a tawny-colored shirt that enhanced the beauty of her eyes.

He nodded and went over to his bag. "If you're ready, I'll call to have our luggage taken downstairs," he said without looking at her.

"I'm ready."

After the call, they awkwardly waited for someone to arrive. Finally he said, "Look, I'm sorry about last night."

She stood at the window looking out. Without turning she said, "I know. I owe you an apology. I've never massaged a man before and...I should have realized that some men might, uh, have a purely physical reaction during a massage."

He frowned. Seated in one of the chairs, he said, "Do you think that's what happened?"

She finally turned and looked at him. "Don't you?"

"No. I think we were responding to the strong attraction we have for each other that's been there like a great big elephant we've been doing our best to ignore."

"Whatever you want to call it, I would prefer that we avoid situations where we might be intimate again." She held her chin high and she spoke firmly. Only her reddened cheeks let him know she was embarrassed.

"Then I owe you an apology. I thought what we were feeling toward each other last night was mutual. I didn't mean to take advantage of you."

She sat on the edge of the bed. "It was mutual. I know that. I'm not trying to put you in a bad light. But I believe we need to put a little distance between us from now on."

"If that would make you more comfortable."

She nodded firmly. "It would."

"So…what do you suggest? Shall I ride in the back seat while you drive?" he asked, trying to hide his amusement at how serious she was.

She closed her eyes briefly and shook her head. "Of course not. It would be wiser to get separate rooms when we stop tonight. You said we should arrive at your home sometime tomorrow." When he started to speak, she said, "I'll be safe enough. There is no way anyone would know where I am at this point."

He shrugged. "If that's what you want."

"Yes, it is."

A knock on the door saved him from having to say anything more. Leslie went to the door and opened it for the bellman. Once they checked out of the hotel and the luggage was in the trunk, Jason said, "We need to eat before we get on the road." He nodded to a Bob Evans restaurant across the street. "They serve excellent breakfasts there, if you'd like to try one."

She drove them across to the parking lot. Once they left the car, Jase noticed that Leslie kept a good three feet away from him at all times, which made him feel like some kind of lecher who preyed on vulnerable women.

His sense of guilt continued to eat at him.

The drive between St. Louis and Dallas was long and uneventful. Leslie focused on driving, going the speed limit as much as possible, leaving Jason too much time to brood. The closer he got to his home, the more depressed he became.

They crossed the Red River into Texas close to eight o'clock that night.

"Why don't you let me drive from here?" he asked. "It isn't more than a couple of hours to Dallas."

She pulled into the parking lot of the visitors' center and stopped. They'd made good time because they hadn't stopped for anything but gas, much as she had done when she'd driven north from Tennessee.

However the tension between them, in addition to the long hours, had taken its toll on Leslie. All she wanted to do was to find a room of her own and curl up into a ball.

Why was it she felt like a fool for being prudent where Jason was concerned? Just because she didn't engage in casual affairs didn't mean there was anything wrong with her. If she'd ever had any concern that perhaps she wouldn't care for an intimate relationship, she'd had that concern erased the night before.

She'd forgotten to be embarrassed. She'd forgotten her upbringing, her caution and her future because she'd been so turned on by touching Jason. All she could think about at the time was making love with him.

Her reaction to Jason had caught her off guard. The truth of the matter was that she no longer trusted herself to be alone with him without doing something foolish she'd live to regret.

The trouble was that she was much too attracted to him and she didn't trust those feelings. She was probably seeing him as some kind of rescuer—which he was—and attributing to him all kinds of honorable traits to him that might not exist.

He'd never given her reason to doubt his word, but she'd never had to trust him in that regard. His behavior at the cabin had been a little off-putting until the night he'd asked her to sleep with him. She'd known that they had both needed the comfort of someone nearby.

Last night was different. Neither one of them had been looking for comfort, but sexual gratification. A relationship simply must be more than that for her to get involved with anyone. From everything he'd told her about himself, he didn't sound like a stable, family man type to her. Not to mention that he was in the military.

She broke the silence by asking, "You've mentioned you have two brothers, Jake and Jude. Do you have any sisters?"

"No sisters. I haven't mentioned Jared, the next to the oldest. There're four of us. We're each two years or so apart."

"Will I be meeting the others? I mean, besides Jake?"

"Maybe. Jared and Lindsey live in Houston. They had a little boy a year ago September. They may come over to visit. I doubt Jude will be there.

"I've already told you about Jake. He runs the ranch. He and Ashley have two children. It doesn't seem possible that their baby, little Joe, will be two in June. Heather, his daughter, will be seven in September. I've never seen little Joe and I bet I won't recognize Heather."

"Do your parents live near the ranch?"

"My folks have a place of their own on the ranch. Now that Dad's retired, they do a great deal of traveling. I understand they're at the ranch now."

"Did you enjoy having a large family?"

"Pretty much. There was always some sibling rivalry going on about something or the other, but nothing serious. I love and admire my brothers."

"You're really fortunate."

"I agree."

When Jason pulled into the driveway of one of the

hotels on the highway in Dallas, the tension between them had eased. Leslie hoped that the awkwardness between them had been smoothed over.

She waited in the car while he went to check in. He took longer than usual and when he came back to the car, he was alone rather than with a bellman.

Leslie rolled her window down. "Is something wrong?"

"There's some kind of big to-do going on here, or maybe a combination of things. Since I didn't call ahead for reservations, we're going to have a little difficulty finding a place to stay. They're booked up here. The concierge called around to several of the hotels on this side of town and found that only one hotel had a room. Since you said you don't want to share a room tonight, we can keep driving for a while longer, if you'd like. We might find something in Arlington or Fort Worth."

Leslie had already been envisioning a long soaking bath after driving all day. The thought of driving any further didn't appeal to her. She sighed. "Let's take whatever's available."

He nodded and got into the car.

"I promise not to come on to you or make you uncomfortable in any way," he said, pulling back out on the access road.

"It isn't *your* behavior I'm concerned about."

Ten

Jase looked at her in astonishment, almost missing the entrance to the expressway. Had she meant that—No, she couldn't have.

"I'm afraid I don't follow you," he said carefully.

"Of course you do. We've been sharing close quarters for several days now and we've been isolated, either in the cabin, the car or a hotel room. We're healthy human beings, which means that I, for one, will continue to be tempted to make love to you as long as we spend our time alone together."

"Oh, man, you could have talked all day without mentioning that particular problem."

"We've got to deal with it."

"Great idea. Let's go ahead and make love and get it out of the way."

She laughed. She actually laughed, when the mere

mention of the possibility had him aching with need. He wanted to make love to her.

Immediately.

If not sooner.

"I don't think that's the solution, Jason."

"Well, if we're going to vote on the matter, that's where my vote's going." He spotted the hotel and signaled to exit the expressway. "I hope they still have the room."

"I'm ready to get out of the car for a few hours."

Oh, there was still a vacancy at the hotel, all right. The only problem, and one Jason hadn't thought to ask about, was that the only room available had one king-size bed.

He went ahead and checked in and hoped to hell to convince her that he hadn't known, especially after the things he'd said coming over here. Once the bellman unloaded their bags from the car, Jase eased himself back into the passenger's seat. "There's another entrance that's closer to our room at the other end of the building."

When they'd parked and reached the hotel door, he slid the card he'd been given into the lock so the door could be opened. "Nice safety feature," he said brusquely, dreading the next few minutes.

"Yes."

Now that she was in the light, he could see how tired she was…drawn and wan from those long hours of driving. Unfortunately he was about to make matters worse.

"Leslie," he said while they waited for the elevator.

"Hmm?" she responded absently, watching the lights indicating the floors flick on and off as the elevator descended.

"There is one thing I haven't mentioned." The ping

of the elevator's arrival stopped him. He waited until they were inside and had punched the button for their floor before he added, "I just want you to know I didn't plan this."

She rested her head against the wall and closed her eyes. "Let me guess. There's a water shortage. No bathing after a certain hour."

"No."

"Good, because I intend to soak in a tub full of warm water for at least an hour."

"The room only has one bed."

Her eyes flew open. "You've got to be kidding."

"No."

"One bed? But that's ridiculous."

"Not really. It's a king size. Couples request them as a rule."

"We're not a couple."

"You know, I believe you're right."

"This isn't funny."

"And I'm not laughing. It isn't as if we haven't slept together before, Leslie—in a bunk bed for one and in a double for another. For that matter, I doubt we'll be able to find each other in a king-size bed."

The elevator doors opened and they stepped out. His leg was hurting like a son of a gun. The last thing he was interested in was making any moves on her tonight.

And who are you kidding? You aren't dead, which is the only way you wouldn't be interested and you know it.

He leaned heavily on the cane as they made their way down the hall. They arrived at the room assigned and he unlocked and opened the door. Leslie went in first and looked around.

"It's really a nice room," she said, peeking into the bathroom.

"It should be, at these prices."

She turned to look at him. "Omigosh. How could I have forgotten to pay for our lodgings?" She picked up her purse from the dresser where she'd laid it. "I can write you a check for our travel expenses right now, although you might have to hold on to it until they're no longer trying to find me."

He didn't need this. "Don't be ridiculous," he said. "I was just making a comment, not trying to get money from you. I'd be spending the same amount of money coming home, anyway."

"Oh."

She turned away and he shook his head. *Way to go, Crenshaw, bite her head off.*

The luggage had been placed on folding luggage racks. "I'll take a shower and get out of your way so you can have your long soak. Believe me, I'll be sound asleep by the time you're ready for bed."

"All right," she said.

He moved toward her and brushed a wisp of hair behind her ear. "This will work out, you'll see."

He knew he was standing too close to her; knew he needed to step back. Instead he brushed his lips across hers in a soft caress. "I can't help wanting to make love to you, Leslie, but I can certainly control my impulses. You're safe with me. I promise."

When he straightened, he saw a tear spill over her lashes. She hastily wiped it away. "I'm just tired. I'll be okay."

Jason showered quickly and returned to the other room. She'd turned out all the lights but one beside the bed. As soon as he walked in, she got up from the chair in which she'd been sitting and went into the bathroom closing the door quietly behind her.

He waited until he heard the gush of water filling the tub before he sat on the side of the bed away from the light. He massaged his thigh in an effort to ease the muscles and eventually stretched out on the bed, pulling the covers over his chest. Within minutes, he was asleep.

Leslie sank into the water with a sigh. It felt just as good as she'd imagined.

She rested her head against the back of the tub and closed her eyes…and immediately saw Jason Crenshaw in her mind. She had learned so much about herself since her placid life had been shattered by the sound of a single shot.

She'd never known so much fear.

She'd never run so far so fast in her life.

She'd never come so close to freezing in a snowstorm.

She'd never met anyone like Jason.

When he wasn't being the most disagreeable person she'd ever met, Jason had an innate charm that showed through his grumpiness and engrained manners that couldn't be disguised. And he was an honorable man. He was honest, too, and made no attempt to hide the fact that he wanted to make love to her. The problem was—and she squirmed at the memory of how he'd caused her to lose control last night—that she wanted to make love to him, too. Despite the sound talking-to she'd given herself, she was ready to ignore all the rules she'd set up for her life.

The time she'd spent with him during the past several days had made her so aware of him—the sound of his breathing…the way his eyes glinted when he looked at her…his rare smile. They all worked to keep him up-permost in her mind.

Well, she had one more night to get through sharing a room with him and sincerely hoped she would show more self-restraint than she had the night before. He'd been right about the bed, after all. They would be a good arm's length away from each other, so it would almost be like sleeping alone. Almost.

Leslie drowsed in the tub until the water cooled off. She felt much more relaxed now and knew she would be able to sleep.

Jason was sound asleep, his head buried beneath his pillow, when she walked into the room. His bare back gleamed in the lamplight. She fought the almost irresistible urge to run her hands along his spine.

With fresh determination she turned off the light so that she could no longer see him and slipped beneath the covers on her side of the bed. Within minutes she was asleep.

Sometime during the night she must have gotten cold and sometime during the night he must have reached for her because when Leslie surfaced from a delicious dream, she discovered she hadn't been dreaming. She and Jason were passionately kissing, their arms and legs tangled with each other.

She gave herself up to all the wonderful sensations he evoked.

Jason's dream became a little too realistic to be a dream. He was in the process of making love to Leslie and she was encouraging him with soft little sounds that added fuel to his already blazing desire.

He lifted his mouth from hers and stopped his hands from stroking her. "Leslie," he began, not certain what to say at this point. A gentleman would never have allowed this to happen, asleep or awake. Hadn't he promised?

She offered him a sleepy smile. "It's all right, Jason. Let's just accept the fact that we're going to do this."

She was right. They'd moved from early foreplay to heavy petting and there was no turning back at this point.

He didn't trust his leg to hold his weight and so he rolled with her in his arms until she lay on top of him. Her pajama bottoms were gone—when had he done that? he wondered—which gave him unfettered access to her. He pushed her hips against him and moved beneath her, making them both groan. He wasn't certain who did what after that, all he knew was that he had slipped between her legs and was probing her. He pushed, feeling the tightness as well as her damp welcome.

He pulled slightly away and surged forward again, moving a little deeper each time until he was fully seated deep inside her.

Jase could no longer control his urgency and he set up a fast rhythm while his thumb played with her sensitive nub until they both cried out in release. His went on and on while he held her tightly against him. She dropped her head to his shoulder and eventually whispered, "I'm too heavy for you."

"Says who?" he murmured.

"I don't want to hurt you."

Lazily he opened his eyes. She lay sprawled against him, her legs on either side of his hips. He kissed her ear and then gently turned until they were facing each other.

"Are you okay?" he finally asked when his breathing calmed down.

"Mmm-hmm."

He had to admit she looked and sounded very content. He was still inside her and still hard, which amazed him. That had never happened before.

He began a slow, rocking movement, which she immediately met, picking up the rhythm. Time disappeared as they whispered and touched and kissed, eventually stepping up the pace until they both experienced another explosive climax.

This time Jason knew he wouldn't be moving anytime soon.

They drifted off to sleep, his arms still wrapped snugly around her.

Eleven

A slight noise awoke Leslie. It was Jason…a dressed Jason…with two extra-large cups of coffee sporting a well-known logo on the side coming through the door. She'd never heard him get up, or dress, or leave, which was unlike her.

She was discovering that her behavior lately was more and more unlike the person she thought she was.

Leslie pushed herself up in bed and grinned at him "Hmm, that smells so good. Thanks for going to get it."

He didn't smile. "I thought we could use some this morning."

He handed her one of them and sat down on her side of the bed, holding his.

"Is something wrong?" she asked.

"Not if you can tell me you're on birth control pills."

She looked at him in growing horror. "Oh, Jason. I'm not. I never expected…" Her voice trailed off.

"Yeah, well, despite all my talk, I wasn't, either. I don't even have any protection with me because I didn't expect to need any while I was at the cabin."

"Well," she said, trying to put the matter in a realistic light. "I really doubt that we could have—"

"When was your last cycle?"

She felt her face heat up. She hadn't given the matter any thought because there'd never been a reason to pay attention. Now she thought back and began to have a sinking feeling in the pit of her stomach.

"About two weeks ago."

He studied her thoughtfully. "So you know what we do now, right?"

After a moment, she slowly nodded her head. "Well, we'll need to wait to find out if—"

"Wrong answer. We're going to take a slight detour this morning to the courthouse, where we'll obtain a license and find a justice of the peace to marry us."

If she hadn't been totally awake before, his words certainly did the trick. "You're kidding, right?"

"No."

"Well, you can forget about playing the martyr where I'm concerned. If there are any repercussions, and at this point there's no way to know, I'll deal with them without your help."

She threw the covers back and got up, marched into the bathroom and shut the door…before she slid down the door to the floor.

She was neither naive nor stupid but, boy, she'd certainly played the role well this morning. This was exactly how teenage girls got pregnant! And she was no teenager.

Now Mr. I'll-Do-The-Right-Thing Crenshaw was

waiting out there ready to give her all his reasons for coming up with his insane idea.

As a matter of fact, he wasn't "Mr." at all. He was a soldier. She didn't know his rank, but he was military through and through. Well, she wanted no part of that kind of life. Sure, he'd said he wouldn't be in combat anymore, as though he had any control over where he was sent. Her father had been in the reserves and that certainly hadn't saved him.

No. She stood and turned on the shower. Her pajama top was the only thing she had on, in case she needed to be reminded of what she'd done.

Leslie didn't care what Jason had to say, the very last thing she was going to do was marry him.

Since she hadn't grabbed any clothes before she'd gone running into the bathroom, Leslie walked out of the bathroom with as much dignity as she could muster wearing nothing but a towel.

He was waiting for her in one of the chairs. His gaze seemed to strip the towel away while he continued to eye her.

She didn't say a word. Instead she gathered her clothes and returned to the bathroom where she took her time getting dressed and readying herself for a battle she couldn't afford to lose.

She didn't care what kind of argument he made; she was not marrying Jason Crenshaw.

He hadn't moved from his chair when she joined him.

She stood across the room from him. "Shall we go have breakfast?" she asked cheerfully.

"No."

"Why not?"

"We're not going anywhere until we settle this matter."

She lifted her chin. "It's settled."

"Good. Then you're going to marry me."

"No! Get it through your thick skull. I. Am. Not. Going. To. Marry. You."

"Hear me out, Leslie, okay? If you refuse my offer, there's no way I can force you. But first, I need to tell you where I'm coming from. First, I have never in my life, not once, forgotten to use protection. Until now." She started to say something and he held up his hand in a stop gesture. "There's something between us and we both know it. I've never wanted anyone like this before and if you find out that you're pregnant, I don't want you to have to 'deal' with it when I might not be around.

"I know we haven't known each other long. I'm well aware of that. I understand your reservations. What I'm proposing is a quick marriage today. If and when you find out you aren't pregnant, and if you want, we can have it annulled."

"A marriage like that is an insult to the institution," she said. "I don't want to get married. When I do decide to marry, it will be to some ordinary guy with an ordinary job who will be content with an ordinary wife."

"There's nothing ordinary about you."

"I especially don't want to marry anyone in the military."

"Because of your dad."

"That's right," she said with a nod.

"Our case is different. I may not stay in the military. I haven't decided, yet."

"I'm also not comfortable with marrying someone who can walk into a dealership and pay cash for an automobile."

"Oh, come on!" Jason's voice rose. "That's the most

asinine reason not to marry someone I've ever heard. At least I know you're not marrying me for my money!"

"Ha. Ha."

"I'm sure you don't care that I already feel lower than a skunk because I'm going to have to face my family in a few hours with no more explanation than I was too busy feeling sorry for myself to think of anybody's feelings but my own!

"Maybe what happened to my squad was beyond my control. However, this—" he waved his hand to her and the bed "—I do have some control over. I refuse to take any chances that I might have gotten you pregnant without making certain that, even at this late date, you're protected. It's going to be tough enough for me to face my family today without knowing that I took advantage of our situation after I promised I wouldn't."

He finished his coffee and waited. When she didn't say anything, he went on. "All right, then. Are you prepared to explain to our child, if there is one, that you chose not to marry his—or her—father because he wasn't what you wanted as a husband?"

The silence became heavy.

"You're not being fair," she finally said.

"And as far as I can see, neither are you."

Leslie couldn't believe she was actually having this conversation with anyone, much less Jason Crenshaw. He was making it sound as though she was the one being irresponsible. Finally she said, "All right, Jason. Here's the deal. If we decide to go through with this farce, it will only be until we know whether or not I'm pregnant."

"And if you are?" he demanded.

She sighed and shook her head.

"I'm not such a bad guy, you know," he said more quietly. "My family will vouch for me. You could do worse."

"Wasn't it just a few days ago when you were laughing about your brothers getting married and you being the lone holdout in the family?"

"So what?"

Sometime during his lecture, she'd sat on the end of the bed, facing him. Now as she looked into his eyes, she could see the hurt and bewilderment in them. So maybe he had a point. All he wanted to do was to protect her. How could she be angry with that?

He certainly hadn't seduced her. She'd as much as spelled out her response to him before they'd checked into the hotel. Maybe she was the one who needed to face the possible results of her own behavior.

She wouldn't have the wedding of her dreams. Well, she should have thought about that before her brain turned off.

"How do you intend to explain a marriage to your family?"

The expression on his face lightened. "Does that mean you're going to consider it?"

"We're both overreacting here, and you know it as well as I do. But for the sake of argument, I would rather be married than have to deal with a possible pregnancy on my own. I just think it would be more sensible to wait and find out before we jump into anything."

"So what you're saying is, you're only willing to marry me if it becomes necessary."

"Jason?"

"Yes?"

"This is cruel and inhumane treatment."

He pulled himself out of the chair and stared at her in astonishment. "Asking you to marry me?"

"No. Having such a serious discussion on an empty stomach. I'm famished."

"All right. Let's go eat."

"Great. And not one word about getting married during the meal. Is it a deal?"

His mouth lifted into a half smile. "You're a tough negotiator."

She nodded. "And don't you forget it."

They stood in line waiting to get a marriage license at the Dallas County courthouse two hours later.

Leslie glanced around at the other couples who looked so excited and happy. When she'd listed all the changes that had taken place in her life lately, she would never have thought to add marriage to the list.

Jason had kept his word over breakfast, but he hadn't eaten much. That's when she realized there was no reason to fight with him. He'd made some excellent points and she'd needed to let go of her childish dreams.

When they reached the clerk, she asked them pertinent questions and typed the answers into the computer. Once the document was ready, Jason asked, "Can we get married now?"

The clerk glanced over her glasses at them. "In a hurry, are you? Sorry, there's a seventy-two-hour wait, unless you're in active military service."

He pulled out his military ID and handed it to her.

She took down the necessary information, clipped her note to the license and gave it to him.

"Next question. Is there a justice of the peace in the building?"

"Several," the clerk drawled.

She gave him directions and they left. Once Jason and Leslie were outside the door, Leslie said, "I bet she thinks I'm pregnant." She knew she sounded disgruntled, but couldn't seem to help it.

"Do you care what she thinks?"

"I don't even know what *I* think, anymore."

He hugged her to him. "It's going to be okay, Leslie."

Jason was in an all-out push to get the matter taken care of as soon as possible. They stopped at one of the judge's offices and were told the judge would be with them shortly.

The actual ceremony was anticlimactic. The judge hastily signed the license and they took it to county records to have it recorded. Jason gave the clerk the ranch address and was told they would receive their copy in a few days.

He took Leslie's hand and they returned to the parking garage where he'd left the car. She offered to drive but he shook his head. He needed to be doing something and concentrating on driving would help.

Without asking, he pulled into a restaurant parking lot and stopped. "I need to eat something."

She glanced at her watch. "No wonder. It's almost twelve."

He nodded and they went inside.

The waitress was friendly and they smiled at her good humor. "You folks on vacation?"

Jason nodded. "I guess you could say that."

"Bet you live around here, don't you, with that drawl."

"The Hill Country."

"Thought as much." She turned to Leslie. "How 'bout you, honey. You a native Texan?"

"I'm afraid not. I'm from—"

Before she could finish her sentence the waitress laughed and said, "The Deep South. I can hear it in your voice. Now then, what would y'all like to eat?"

Now that he'd gotten the marriage out of the way, Jason was hungry and decided on the buffet while Leslie chose the salad bar.

Once the waitress left, Leslie said, "She's a character, isn't she?" sounding amused.

"Lots of 'em around, so you'd better get used to it."

"I've never been to Texas. I think I mentioned that to you."

He nodded and smiled. "Well, you're in Texas now, honey, where the men are men and the women are glad of it."

She laughed. "And the men are also modest."

"I like your laugh," he said. "Have I told you that?"

She glanced away before meeting his eyes. "No, you never have."

"Guess I haven't heard you laugh much since I've known you."

"For good reason."

"Well, you're safe now. You're officially a Crenshaw of Texas and nobody's going to bother you again." He stood. "Getting married seems to have whet my appetite," he said, and laughed when she just looked at him.

Leslie kept her attention on the surrounding scenery as they drove into the Hill Country, not wanting to dwell on the fact that Jason hadn't said a word during the past three hours. They'd left the interstate about an hour ago and now followed a two-lane highway west.

The sun kept playing peek-a-boo with the clouds and

by the time they reached the entrance to the ranch, there
was little light left in the sky.

Leslie looked at the stonework on either side of the
wide entrance. It was quite elegant. The wrought-iron
fence stood open and they passed over a cattle guard into
the actual ranch. She was in real cowboy country now.

"You okay? Haven't heard anything from you for a
while." She turned and looked at him. His face looked
drawn and he was pale. "You're hurting, aren't you?"

One corner of his mouth lifted slightly. "That obvious, is it?"

"Once we get there, you're going to take one of your
pain pills, like it or not," she said fiercely.

He did a double take. "Haven't been married to you
but a few hours and already you're bossing me around!"

She took a deep breath to reply when she saw his eyes
twinkling. He was teasing her. She was going to have
to get used to his sense of humor.

"If you take your meds, I'll give you a massage," she
offered slyly.

"You're on, lady."

The ranch road wound through the hills. She saw
huddled herds of cows and sheep...and weren't those
things goats over there?

"Oh! Look, there's a deer!" she said with excitement.

"Honey, we've got more deer around here than livestock. They're pests."

"But they're so beautiful and so graceful."

"And hungry. The women on the ranch have to put
up barriers if they want to have any kind of garden.
Otherwise, the deer help themselves to everything."

"Are they tame?"

"Most of them aren't. I remember when I was a kid

that one of the ranch hands found a fawn near its mother that had been killed. He brought it back and raised it at his place. It was the darndest thing. That deer followed him around like a dog. He said she slept beside his bed at night because he wouldn't let her get on it like she wanted."

"You're teasing me."

"Nope. Ask Jake, or anyone who lives on the ranch, for that matter. I bet Ashley remembers Conchita. Miguel was proud of that deer."

Leslie lost track of the conversation when they came up on a rise and she looked down into a wide expanse of valley. The large house looked like something from a movie set. It was huge, with a red-tiled roof and white walls. From here, she could see patios on several sides of the house. With the many barns and sheds nearby, the place looked like a village.

"Oh, it's so beautiful," she said.

"It's home," Jason replied, sounding gruff.

When they got closer Jason pulled around to the side of the house and parked.

He turned to look at her. With a rueful smile, Jason said, "Welcome to the ancestral home of the Crenshaws."

Twelve

"It's about time you showed up, fella. I was about ready to form a search party to look for you!"

Leslie and Jason had just gotten out of the car when she heard the deep male voice. She glanced over the roof of the car and saw a big man with broad shoulders, lean hips and long legs loping toward them from one of the patios.

She watched as he reached Jason's side. "You doin' okay?" she heard him ask Jason in a low voice.

Jason nodded. "Just tired."

Leslie walked around the car toward the two men. "Because he refused to let me drive and give his leg a rest," she added. She held out her hand. "Hi, I'm Leslie O'Brien and I have a hunch you're Jake."

Jake looked startled and she wondered why.

"I'm pleased to meet you, Ms. O'Brien. Seems

Jase forgot to mention a couple of things when he spoke to Jude."

"Oh? I thought you knew I was coming with him," she replied, feeling awkward.

"Oh, sure, Jude told me about that part. He just forgot to mention that you happened to be young, attractive and can hold your own with our boy, here." He turned to Jason. "I'll get your luggage. You two get on in the house where it's warm."

Jason moved slowly toward the patio. Once they reached it, Leslie could see into the house because of a large picture window next to the door. Jake was there before either one of them could reach for the door. He set their luggage down and pushed open the door.

"There you go."

Leslie stepped inside first and looked around. She was in a large, airy kitchen with a table and chairs at one end and all the modern conveniences a cook could need or want. She turned and looked at Jason. "Your cabin could fit inside this kitchen without touching a thing."

He sat down. "I know."

"Can I get you something?" Jake asked, looking at his brother with worried eyes.

"He needs to take his meds. He's too macho and stubborn to take them without being browbeaten."

"Hey!" Jason said sternly. "I resent that remark!"

"Where are they?" Jake asked tersely.

"In my shaving kit in my bag," Jason replied wearily.

Jake found the bottle and handed it to Jason, got a glass, filled it with water and brought it back to Jason. "Take one."

Leslie waited for an argument that never happened. Without a word, Jason took the pill.

They both stood watching him. He looked at first one and then the other and shook his head. "I'm going to be fine, okay?" He looked at Jake. "Where are Ashley and the kids?"

"Ashley took Heather and Joey down to the folks, where they'll be spending the night. We figured you might need a little peace and quiet when you first got here."

Leslie watched the brothers exchange a long look of silent communication.

"I'm a little surprised that the folks are home, the way Dad likes to travel," Jason said after a moment.

Jake grinned. "Dad's about given up trying to get Mom to make any long trips with him since the children arrived. Finding out she had a three-year-old granddaughter she didn't know about changed her views on traveling pretty fast when Heather first arrived. Then when Joey came, Dad said it would take a crowbar bigger than he could handle to pry her away from here."

"I'm looking forward to getting acquainted with my nephew. I bet he's really grown."

"Too fast, as far as I'm concerned. This time last year Joey was barely crawling. Now we have to watch him like a hawk because he's always on the go." Jake turned to Leslie. "Sorry, didn't mean to ignore you. Have a seat and let me get you something to drink."

She smiled. "Actually, I was wondering if you could show me the room where I'll be staying. I'd like to freshen up and I know you two have lots to catch up on."

Jake nodded. "Sure." He picked up her luggage. "I'll show you to your room."

Leslie followed him up a gracefully curving staircase and down a hallway. He stopped and opened one of the doors. "Hope you find the room comfortable."

She could only stare. The room was almost as large as her entire apartment. "It's lovely," she finally managed to say.

"Good. Take your time. We'll be eating in another hour or so. Feel free to rest for a while."

"Thank you," she said faintly, and watched as he went out of the room.

When Jason had spoken of his home Leslie had imagined an old farmhouse sitting in the middle of nowhere. She certainly hadn't pictured anything like this Spanish-style home the size of a hotel!

She shivered. Her life was becoming stranger by the minute. She was married to a man who appeared to have untold resources at his fingertips and who had a brother with untold resources in law enforcement. He'd mentioned that Jake was in charge of the ranch. If the drive to the main house was any indication, the place was huge.

She opened her luggage and pulled out one of her dresses. She wondered if Jason would mention to Jake that they were married.

She and Jason hadn't touched on the subject once they headed south, which was just as well. She didn't want to say any more that could hurt Jason, and whether he would admit it or not, he'd been hurt when she'd first refused to marry him.

He was a strange mixture of toughness and tenderness, of grumpiness and charm, and she was never certain how he'd react to something she might say.

The fact was that the deed was done. No need for more discussion. She rather hoped that Jason would keep the marriage to himself.

* * *

"What do you mean, you're married!" Jake said in a deep rumble downstairs in the kitchen.

Jason looked at his older brother and already wished that he'd kept his mouth shut, at least for a while. "Could we have this discussion in another room so I can get a little more comfortable?"

"Don't change the subject." Jake stood and walked to the door into the foyer. Jason stood and realized that the pain meds were already doing their job. He felt a little light-headed, but getting some relief was worth it.

Once he was stretched out in one of the recliners in the living room, Jason sighed and said, "Just what I said. Leslie and I were married in Dallas this morning, which is why we got here later than I expected. I didn't think our arrival time mattered, so I didn't think about calling you."

Jake ignored the explanation and went back to the information that had caught him by surprise. "You married her after you've known her for—how long—a week?"

"Jake, not everybody has to know the woman they marry from her birth, like you did with Ashley."

"Never said they did. But this is so unlike you, impulsively making a serious commitment like marriage. But then, hiding out in the northern woods without telling anybody you'd been wounded isn't what I would have expected from you, either. So what's going on with you?"

Jason leaned back in his chair and stretched his arms above his head. "Sure good to be back home. It's so peaceful, so serene, so restful."

"All right, you've made your point." Jake was quiet for a moment. "I put Leslie in one of the guest rooms. Guess I should have put her in your room. You should have said something earlier."

"You did just fine. I probably won't be sleeping with her, anyway."

Jake stared blankly at Jason for several minutes before he threw up his hands. "I refuse to ask any more questions…about your personal life, anyway. Tell me what happened to you." He nodded toward Jason's leg.

He listened intently as Jason forced himself to relive his nightmare one more time.

When Leslie ventured downstairs almost an hour later, she heard voices coming from a room off the main foyer. Recognizing that one of the voices was Jason's, she walked to the archway and paused, looking at yet another large room filled with comfortable furniture and a gigantic television screen at one end.

Before any of the occupants saw her, Leslie noticed a woman who must be Ashley seated next to Jake on one of the long sofas. Jake glanced up and saw her. He immediately stood.

"Come on in, Leslie, and meet Ashley, my wife."

Ashley stood and offered a sparkling smile. "I'm so glad Jason brought you with him." She took her hand and gently squeezed it. "I know this must be a really scary time for you. I can't imagine what I'd do in your circumstances."

Leslie shrugged and smiled. "I just happened to be in the wrong place at the wrong time. It could have happened to anyone working in my building. That's what I get for staying late to catch up on my work."

Ashley shuddered. "Well, at least you found Jason hibernating up north. I'm glad Jude suggested the two of you come here." She motioned to a chair near Jason, who was comfortably sprawled in a recliner. "Have a seat," she said. "Dinner will be ready in a few minutes. Nothing fancy, I'd better warn you. A casserole one of the wives here on the ranch put in the freezer for us. We'd probably starve to death if it were left up to me."

Jake lifted an eyebrow. "Now tell her why."

Ashley shrugged. "I'm one of the local veterinarians and even when I'm supposed to be home, I'm generally on call for emergencies."

Leslie looked at her in amazement. "You don't look like any vet I ever met," she said, and sat down. She looked at Jason. "How are you feeling?"

"Better."

"The pain has eased, then."

"Took the edge off." The look he gave her stole her breath. "I've never seen you in a dress before," he said quietly.

"It was too cold until now."

"You look good," he murmured as though they were alone in the room.

She looked away. "Thank you."

"So," Ashley said, probably in an effort to change the subject, "Jason's been telling us about your busy day…getting married in the morning…driving for the rest of the day…and now spending your wedding night with his family. He's such a romantic, as I'm sure you've already discovered."

Leslie looked at Jason and in a low voice said, "I didn't know you were going to tell them."

He frowned. "Why wouldn't I? Did you want to keep it a secret?"

"I've already read him the riot act," Ashley continued. "The license is good for several weeks. Y'all could have waited and married here, with family."

Jason smiled. "I liked our wedding just fine. No fuss."

"Did you bother asking Leslie how she felt about a hurry-up wedding?"

Leslie immediately answered, hoping to circumvent anything Jason might say. "I didn't mind. It was all very sudden."

"I'd have to agree with that," Jake drawled, watching his brother with amusement.

Ashley spoke up. "The folks will bring Heather and Joey back tomorrow in time to have dinner with us. We didn't want to swamp you with family all at once."

Jason asked, "Do I need to ask about Mom and Dad's reaction to my 'hibernation,' as you put it?"

Jake replied. "They might surprise you. They were more concerned to hear you'd been hurt than that you hadn't come home immediately. Mom said she's glad to know you survived."

"Guess that puts things into perspective for all of us," Ashley added.

Leslie sat quietly as she listened and watched Jason's family interact with one another. So this was what having family meant. Her mother would have loved it.

During a lull in the conversation, Jason reached over and took her hand. "Is your room okay?"

She smiled. "It's beautiful."

"Good."

"If you'll excuse me," Ashley said, hopping up, "I'll get supper on the table." She grabbed Jake's hand and yanked on it, almost pulling him off the sofa. He glanced at Jason and Ashley, and grinned. "Guess I'm needed in the kitchen. See how subtly Ashley lets me know?"

Once they were alone, Jason said, "What's wrong, Leslie?"

She shook her head. "I'm just tired."

"I never thought to ask what kind of wedding you'd wanted to have. I just wanted to get it done before you backed out on me." He watched her closely. "I owe you an apology."

"It's over and done with. There's no need to rehash everything."

"You're still upset," he said in a level tone.

"I'll get over it. Like I said. I'm tired. Things will look better in the morning, I'm sure."

"I wanted you to be safe, Leslie, in every way. Now I have the legal right to make certain you are."

Jake paused in the doorway. "C'mon, guys. We'll get you fed and let you get some rest. You'll need all you can get before our hellions arrive tomorrow."

Jason's parents. She wondered what they were going to think about their youngest son marrying a stranger—and one who was in danger, no less.

She chuckled as she stood and waited for Jason. He picked up his cane, and as they started toward the kitchen, he asked, "What's so funny?"

She shook her head. "I told you I was tired. I happened to wonder what your parents are going to think about you marrying a stranger in danger." She bit her lip to keep from laughing. At this point, the laughter could quickly turn into hysteria.

"Stranger in danger. I kind of like that. As for my parents, they're going to love you. You know why?"

She shook her head.

"Because you were just what the doctor should have ordered for me all along. I'm glad you came into my life, Leslie. They'll be happy that meeting you has made me happy. We'll get through this together."

Thirteen

The meal was low-key. And delicious. Leslie liked Jake and Ashley. They were a devoted couple, which touched her heart. She listened as the men talked about the ranch, what Jake was doing with various livestock and what the rest of the family was doing.

She could see the strong bond between the brothers. Jason looked more relaxed than she'd ever seen him. And happy. Although he had dreaded the ordeal of coming home and facing them, Jason obviously dearly loved his family.

Did he know how lucky he was?

After supper she excused herself and went upstairs. It didn't take her long to get ready for bed and she was almost asleep when she heard a soft tap on the door.

"Who is it?"

"Me," Jason said softly.

Of course he would sleep in here. There was no rea-son for him not to. "Come in."

She sat up in bed as he stepped inside the room. His hair looked damp from his shower and he wore only a pair of jeans that were unbuttoned at the top.

Jason stood by the door as though hesitating to come any farther. "I, uh, wondered if you could work on my back some."

"You don't have your cane."

He shrugged. "The meds work wonders."

He hadn't intended to sleep with her at all! She al-most laughed at her assumption that he was eager to make love to her again.

"Of course," she replied. "Come lie on the bed."

He sat on the side of her bed to remove his jeans and she realized he wore nothing underneath. She shouldn't be shocked by his nonchalance, but this being married to him was going to take some adjustments in her thinking.

He rolled over onto his stomach and stretched out next to her. She began to knead his back.

"Leslie?"

"Hmm?"

"I railroaded you into this marriage and I know it. You said the only reason you would agree is if the mar-riage was temporary."

"Mmm-hmm."

"So I don't want you to think that I'm going to take advantage of the fact that I can legally sleep with you, because I'm not. You probably don't believe I can keep a promise, but this one I'll swear an oath to. I won't make love with you or sleep in your bed until and un-less I'm invited."

"You're sounding pretty humble for a Texas male."

"I'm serious."

"All right."

"Once the men who committed the murder are convicted, I want you to feel free to get on with your life without my hanging around."

Each sentence had been accompanied by a moan of pleasure as she worked the kinks out of his back.

"Okay."

He stiffened, raised his head and looked around at her. "Okay?" he repeated, sounding disgruntled.

"I appreciate your understanding. Hopefully, I'll be able to go home in the not-too-distant future and be able to get a perspective on my life."

He dropped his head into the pillow. "Great," she thought he said, but the pillow muffled the word.

Jason had a beautiful body and she loved touching him. There were many things she loved about him, one of them being his sense of honor. Regardless of how she felt about him, she reminded herself, they were a total mismatch.

She'd been rather sheltered and had been content with her uneventful life.

He was a highly skilled military man who'd traveled extensively and had experienced a life she could scarcely imagine. He wouldn't have run from the scene of a murder.

Just because she was strongly attracted to him and he was the first man to make love to her should not influence her decision about the future. She needed to think with her head and not be so quick to follow her emotions.

Being honest with herself, Leslie knew that if Jason was in love with her and wanted a future together, she'd feel differently about their situation.

Of course that wasn't the case. He'd been alone for a long time and she had shown up at a time when he'd been vulnerable. As vulnerable in his own way as she was. What had occurred between them had been predictable, given their circumstances. If they had used protection this morning, there would never have been mention of a marriage.

She sighed and realized that Jason had fallen asleep. In her bed. Again. After he made a solemn oath not to. He was not going to be very happy with himself when he woke up.

That told her she knew him better than she'd thought.

She stretched out beside him and arranged the covers over him, as well, but it was a long time before she fell asleep.

Jason woke with a start. What was he doing wrapped around Leslie, holding her clutched to him as though afraid she'd disappear out of his life? With stealthy movements, he carefully released her and slid away. She stirred and mumbled something but didn't wake up.

Be thankful for small favors, Crenshaw, you idiot.

He must have fallen asleep while she'd worked on his back last night. He gave his head a quick shake and got out of bed. He fumbled with the jeans he'd left on the floor and quietly made his way to the door.

He opened it and slipped through, silently shutting the door behind him. It was still early. He'd go to his room and grab a few more—

"You're not sleeping with her, huh?" Jake said, striding toward him from the master bedroom and startling Jason out of ten years of his life.

He spun around and grabbed the wall to keep from

falling. "It isn't what it looks like." He limped beside Jake until Jason reached his bedroom.

Jake paused. "Of course not."

"She gave me a massage last night."

"Is that what they're calling it these days?"

"Nothing happened! I fell asleep until just now. Now if you'll excuse me, I guess I'll get dressed since you're up."

"Suit yourself. No need to stay up on my account," Jake replied, and continued down the hallway.

Jason watched his brother walk away and shook his head. Guess it didn't matter how old he was, he would still feel the need to answer to his big brother.

After he dressed and retrieved his cane Jason went downstairs to the kitchen where Jake stood against one of the counters and sipped a cup of coffee. "Help yourself," he said.

While Jason poured himself a cup, Jake asked, "When do you report back to your unit?"

"Once I check in with the doctors at Bethesda and they give me permission."

"Were you kidding when you said you might get out of the service?"

"Nope. I'm considering all my options. Regardless of what the doctor says, this leg will never be the same. I can't trust it not to go out from under me when I really need it."

"What will you do after that?" Jake asked.

"Good question. I don't have many skills that are useful in civilian life."

"Have you thought about coming home and ranching? I know of a place that's up for sale, in case you're interested."

Jason hadn't seen that one coming!

"I know you used to enjoy working with me when you were a kid," Jake added thoughtfully.

"You weren't so old, yourself. Remember, there's only eight years between us."

"And you've been gone for the past twelve."

Jason studied his coffee. He finished what was left and poured another cup. "I needed to grow up and I figured the army was the best way to do it."

"Well, now that you have a wife, you might want to think about settling down here in the Hill Country."

Jason sighed. "It's not a real marriage."

"Oh?"

"Well, I mean it's legal and all that. But we're certainly not in love with each other."

Jake laughed and reached for the coffeepot.

Irritated by Jake's amusement, Jason asked, "What's so funny?"

"You are. I may not have seen much of you in recent years but I know you well enough to know you have strong feelings for Leslie. You light up whenever she walks into the room. You can't keep your eyes off her and if last night was any indication, I'd say that you can't keep your hands off her, either."

"I did not make love to Leslie last night," Jason said through gritted teeth.

"Wanted to, though."

Jason stared at him and a lengthy silence filled the room. Finally he sipped his coffee and said, "That's true enough."

"So what are you doing? Playing some kind of knight with her? You rescued her, you fell in love with her, you married her. Now you won't touch her?"

"It's complicated and I'm not in love with her!"

"So you keep saying."

"It's the truth."

"Fine." Jake put his cup down and straightened. "That leg of yours well enough to straddle a horse?"

"I don't know, but I could try, I suppose."

"Then c'mon and we'll find a docile gelding for you. Let me show you some of the things I've been doing around here lately."

When Leslie woke up she saw that Jason had left sometime during the night. She sighed. The really weird thing was that she'd grown used to sharing a bed with him in—what?—a week. Her emotions were all in a whirl and she wished she could call Teri to discuss things with her. Wouldn't Teri be shocked to hear that she'd married "the soldier"?

However, Jason had cautioned her against the idea, just to be on the safe side and she knew he was right.

Once up and dressed, Leslie went downstairs. She could smell bacon and coffee and her stomach growled in anticipation.

"Good morning," Ashley said as soon as she saw her. "You're right on time. I've already called the guys to say we're eating in a few minutes. I have a hunch they'll show up with big appetites."

"The guys?"

"Jake and Jason. When I called Jake on his cell phone, he said he and Jason rode out to look at some of the new breeding stock Jake brought in a few weeks ago."

"Rode out? Are you saying that Jason's on a horse?"

"So I understand."

"His leg must be better."

As Ashley placed heaping plates of food on the table, Leslie heard footsteps on the patio outside. The door opened and Jake stepped inside, followed by Jason. Her eyes widened. The resemblance between them was remarkable, partly because Jason was wearing boots and a Western hat in addition to his jeans and fleece-lined jacket, the same kind of clothes Jake had on.

His eyes avoided hers. "Mornin'," he said, giving her a quick nod.

The men washed up at the sink and sat across from each other. Leslie took the chair next to Jason.

"You sleep okay?" he asked, passing her a plate of hash brown potatoes.

"Fine, thanks," she said, giving him a quick look before accepting the plate. Bacon and sausage, scrambled eggs and biscuits soon followed.

Jason looked at Ashley, who was seated next to Jake. "Do you have to work today?"

"Not officially. I hope to take this week off. The office crew has promised not to call me unless there's a catastrophe."

"When are the folks coming up?"

Jake glanced at his watch. "In about an hour."

"You told them I got in, right?"

Jake frowned. "They know you were due to arrive. Didn't you call them last night?"

"Forgot."

Jake shook his head. "You're making points in this family as fast as you can."

"I wasn't in the mood to get into a long discussion last night."

"You don't look like you're in a much better mood this morning."

Leslie unobtrusively placed her hand on Jason's thigh and he looked at her sharply. "They love you, Jason," she said. "Be thankful your parents are still alive."

As though they were alone, he brought her hand up to his mouth and kissed it. "Thanks for the reminder," he replied softly before he continued to eat.

"Have you talked to Jude?" Jake asked after breakfast.

"Not since yesterday morning. He said he'd call here this morning with an update. It seems the two deputies continue their rounds with impunity, ostensibly looking for the missing man."

Jake shook his head in disgust and then looked at Leslie. "Would you like to go riding with us?" he asked. "We won't go far."

She looked at him in horror. "On a horse?"

"I take it you haven't been on a horse before," he replied dryly.

She glanced at Jason. "Are you going back out?"

"Probably so. It's a beautiful day. Not much breeze, plenty of sunshine. If you bundle up, you'll be fine."

A horse. The closest she'd been to horses was watching them in the Fourth of July parade each year.

She swallowed and then lifted her chin. "I'd like that if one of you can teach me how to ride without falling off!"

Leslie couldn't believe it. She sat on a horse, despite her fear. She looked around at the two brothers, one on each side of her. "Okay. I'm ready."

Jason said, "Loosen your grip on the reins. She'll stay with us without prompting."

Leslie grabbed the saddle horn with both hands at her horse's first step and hung on as the three horses walked away from the corral. Jason had already taught her how to use her knees to grip and her shoes were firmly in the stirrups. Several minutes passed before she realized that she was enjoying herself.

"You okay?" Jason asked, keeping his mount close to her.

"I think so, at least for now. Who knows what will happen if she goes any faster."

Jake laughed. "You're doing fine, Leslie. I admire your willingness to try new things." He glanced at Jason before continuing. "See that group of trees over there? That's where we're headed. There's something I want to check on."

She saw a windmill near the trees. She smiled. "I'm glad I came with you."

Jason murmured, "So am I." When she looked at him he was smiling. She loved his smile and the way it flashed white in his tanned face.

When they reached the windmill, the men dismounted. Jason lifted Leslie as though she were a lightweight and set her on the ground. She rubbed her bottom.

"Are you getting sore?"

"A little."

"Actually, so am I. I haven't been on a horse in a long time."

"You look so natural riding."

"That's not surprising. Dad had me sitting on a horse in front of him before I could walk."

"You look happy," Leslie said as Jason's gaze wandered over the terrain.

He nodded. "It's good to be home."

"Then you aren't sorry that you brought me here."

He looked at her for a long moment and said, "I'm

not sorry for anything that's happened since you arrived on my doorstep."

So much had happened, but from the look in his eyes, he was recalling making love to her. She glanced away. "Me, either."

Nobody spoke on the way back to the barn. Leslie was nervous about meeting Jason's parents. Finally, when they were at the barn, she asked, "Are you going to tell your parents we're married?"

"Jake and I talked about that earlier. I think I've done enough to upset them without telling them we married suddenly without letting anyone know."

"Good," she said, relief flooding her. "We can save that news for some other time."

Once they dismounted, Jake turned the horses over to one of the stable hands, who would rub them down and feed them. Halfway to the house, Jake said, nodding toward a big, shiny red pickup truck coming toward them, "I told you they wouldn't be long getting here."

"I see Dad got a new truck," Jason said, adjusting his hat and pulling the brim down to shade his eyes.

"Yep."

"Looks good."

"Yep."

Jason punched Jake in the arm. "I get the feeling you had a hand in that."

"Maybe. I told him his old truck was going to collapse into a pile of rust one of these days. Once he saw the new double cabs he decided he might try one. Said he needed the extra seat for the grandkids."

The three of them reached the house at the same time as the truck. Joe got out, holding Joey, and Gail helped Heather down from the truck. Heather saw Jake and came running. "Daddy!" She hugged him tightly around the waist. "I missed you so much!"

He cupped her head with his fingers. "I missed you, too, darlin'."

Jason limped toward his parents. Gail's eyes shone with tears.

"Welcome home, son," Joe said as the three of them met. Gail threw her arms around Jason's neck. "I don't care how old you get," she said fiercely. "You'll always be my baby!"

Joe handed Joey to Gail and pulled Jason into his embrace.

Leslie had tears in her eyes from watching the reunion. Joe Crenshaw was a handsome man with a beautiful wife. The three of them, Joe, Gail and Jason, talked for a while before Joe said, "Are we going to stand here all day?"

Joey wriggled in Gail's arms and leaned toward Jake, who took him with a laugh. The little boy looked just like his daddy. He was patting Jake's cheeks and chattering, while Jake listened and nodded as though he could understand every word.

As the group started to the house, Jason turned to Leslie and held out his hand to her. "Mom, Dad, this is Leslie. She'll be staying with us for a while."

Gail smiled and said, "Welcome, Leslie. I'm so glad that Jason brought you with him. We've got to keep the numbers balanced or these guys get way above themselves."

Joe nodded. "Can't argue with that. Glad to meet you, Leslie. I understand you're in a little trouble and need somewhere to hide. You couldn't have picked a better place."

"Thank you, Mr. Crenshaw. I appreciate everyone's hospitality."

"The name's Joe." He looped his arm around his wife's shoulders. "And this is Gail."

Leslie smiled. "All right."

Jason stood back to let the rest of them go inside and Leslie waited beside him. "Your parents seem like wonderful people," she whispered.

"Of course I'm a little prejudiced, but I think they're pretty special."

Jason's parents left at dark and Jake and Ashley went upstairs to bathe the children and get them ready for bed. Jason turned on the television and motioned Leslie to join him.

"This is a luxury. I can't remember the last time I watched TV," Jason said, choosing the sofa so they could sit together.

"I'm in awe of your family. Are your other brothers as friendly and outgoing as your dad and Jake?"

"I suppose so. Haven't given the matter much thought."

"Your mom said that she has five grandchildren since the twins arrived. She thought she'd give Jude and Carina a chance to settle in with their babies before she went to visit."

"Jude apologized for not calling earlier today. The little guys had actually let them sleep and he ended up late for work."

Being this close to Jason made her want to throw herself into his arms. She was rapidly becoming addicted to having him near.

Later he went upstairs with her and walked her to her

room, where he paused and looked at her. "You fit into this family as if you've always been a part of it." He cupped her face with his hands and brushed his lips over hers. "I've been wanting to do this all day." He kissed her again, pulling her against him until their bodies touched from shoulders to knees. "You're the perfect height for me. See how well we fit together?" he whispered, nibbling on her ear and kissing her jaw.

Leslie couldn't remember a single reason not to invite him into her bed. Well, maybe one. "Did you by any chance acquire protection since yesterday?"

His grin was mischievous. "You betcha. Does that mean you're inviting me to make love to you? Remember, it's your choice."

"I'd like that," she responded, suddenly feeling shy.

Within minutes they were undressed and in bed while Jason showed her how varied, and exciting, lovemaking could be.

He couldn't seem to get enough of her and she enjoyed every minute of it. They didn't fall asleep until the early hours of the next morning.

Fourteen

"**H**ey, Lenny?"

"What, Bryce! Damn it, you woke me up."

"We've got a lead on that witness."

"No kidding. Where is she?"

"Well, she's done gone and got herself a marriage license in Dallas. Don't that beat all?"

"How the hell did she get from Michigan to Texas without us finding her? The man who brought the rental back said he didn't know who we were talking about. Insists he never saw a woman. Said he'd been told to return the car by some man who didn't give his name. I don't know how we could have lost her so completely."

"Yeah, I know. There's no telling. But the computer turned up her name during a search. When I pulled up the document to see if it's the same woman, the address she gave was Deer Creek. It's got to be her, I tell you."

"Who's the guy?"

"The license says his name is Jason Crenshaw. Mean anything to you?"

"No."

"Me, neither."

"Does it give his address?"

"Some post office box in a town called New Eden, Texas, wherever that is."

"We're about to find out. Tell the sheriff we've got a new lead and we're going to take care of a few loose ends."

Two weeks after they arrived Leslie came out of her bathroom and saw Jason propped up in bed, waiting for her.

"You all right?" he asked.

She nodded, feeling a whirl of conflicting emotions. "I'm not pregnant." She crawled back under the covers.

"Oh. Well. That's good. I guess. I mean, it will simplify things."

She curled her knees into her chest.

"Can I get something for you?"

She tried to smile, but it was difficult not to burst into tears, which was ridiculous. She was relieved not to be pregnant. She really was.

"I don't suppose you have a heating pad handy."

He tossed back the covers and grabbed his jeans. "Hold on. I'll be right back."

When the door clicked behind him, Leslie thought about the past couple of weeks. Since Jason had been sleeping with her every night, it was understandable that their marriage had become more real to her.

His leg was mending enough that he no longer used

a cane. It was as though he wanted to get better in a hurry so that he could return to active duty.

And why not?

So. She would return to Deer Creek, hopefully soon, and Jason would go back to his life.

Forgetting him would be impossible. She adored his family and enjoyed playing with the children. Jake's daughter, Heather, was a delight. She was bright, curious, and she never stopped talking. It was Heather who was teaching Leslie all about ranch life each afternoon after Heather came home from school.

Joey was all strutting male, a definite Crenshaw. He stayed with his grandmother, Gail, while Ashley worked.

An extended family was a wonderful gift. She barely remembered her grandparents. Her grandmother died when Leslie was five and her grandfather a little more than a year later.

The bedroom door swung open. Jason unwrapped a heating pad, plugged it into the wall outlet near the bed and handed it to her.

"Thanks," she said, adjusting the heat and hugging the warmth.

"Would you like some coffee? I could bring you some."

"Jason, you don't have to look after me. I'll be fine. The first day is usually the roughest."

He sat beside her and brushed her hair from her forehead. "I hate to see you in pain."

"It's not so bad. More uncomfortable than anything else."

"Has it always been this bad?"

She nodded. "The doctor said I'd probably have less trouble once I have a baby."

They looked at each other in silence. Finally, Jason said, "I'll go get the coffee." He was back with the coffee in a few minutes, hovered until she told him not to be concerned about her, then left.

After the coffee, Leslie curled up beneath the covers and fell back to sleep.

Jake was in the kitchen when Jason returned downstairs. He took one look at his brother's face and said, "Is everything okay?"

Jason nodded. "Leslie's a little under the weather. She said she has trouble every month."

"Well, that shoots my theory. I thought she was pregnant. That was the only reason I could think of for you to jump into marriage."

"Even I'm not good enough to get her pregnant in a week."

"Were you hoping she was pregnant?"

Jason turned away and filled a coffee cup. "Of course not."

"So how, exactly, does this marriage that isn't a real marriage work? You've certainly got me confused."

"I wanted to have the legal right to protect her, even if it was no more than giving her my name."

"I'm impressed. What an honorable thing to do."

Jason turned and faced his brother. "Not so honorable. I wanted to sleep with her and figured this was the only way to do it."

Jake chuckled. "That sounds more like the brother I know and love. You going out with me and the crew today, or do you plan to stay around the house?"

"I'll be ready to go as soon as I get dressed."

After he dressed, Jason peeked into Leslie's bedroom, saw that she was asleep and silently closed the door. He wondered why he had such a hollow feeling in his chest. She would remain here at the ranch for as long as she needed to and he'd go back to Bethesda for his medical release and return to his unit.

He didn't need to leave the army. He'd just needed some time to heal and get his thinking straight.

A marriage between them would never have worked.

Leslie felt much better when she woke up later. It was almost eleven. Everybody would be gone by now. The brothers would be out working somewhere on the ranch and Ashley would be at her office in New Eden.

She got dressed and went downstairs. Ashley had left a note suggesting various things for her to eat. It was almost like having a big sister.

Jude called after she ate and she chatted with him for a while.

"So everybody's left you by yourself today," he commented.

"That's right. You talk to me or nobody."

He laughed. "How do you like the ranch?"

"I'm really enjoying my stay here. I never knew such a place could exist in our modern world. The wide-open spaces amaze me. The business of raising livestock and having roundups here has been going on for a hundred years or more. The continuity is something to be proud of."

"Do you think you'd get tired of the isolation?"

"I don't feel isolated, so it would be difficult to say."

"I don't know if anyone told you about Jake's first wife. She was definitely a city girl. She'd always lived in Dallas and had an active social life. She couldn't stand living on the ranch, which is why she left him."

"She was an idiot. I would think being married to a Crenshaw male would be enough to make any woman happy."

"I think I'll have you talk to my wife and remind her of that. I'll tell her how grateful she should be for the privilege of getting up at night every few hours to feed the latest little Crenshaws. Or maybe not. Her sense of humor has been slipping lately."

"Thank you for sending me here, Jude. I've enjoyed it."

"I'm glad to hear that because things are heating up in Deer Creek, which is why I called. There have been a few arrests, a couple of gambling places have shut down and the lowlife is going to ground. The Bureau says they may need you to testify and they need you somewhere safe. So you might as well settle in and enjoy yourself."

She sighed. "I'm sure my job is long gone. I really feel badly about that."

"Who knows? Once your boss finds out why you left and why you didn't return after a few days, he'll probably rehire you. The honest folk in town are going to be relieved to have the criminal element out of there." He paused and then said, "Tell Jason I called. Everything seems to be moving according to plan."

"I'll tell him."

When the phone rang a half hour later, Leslie looked at it in surprise. The phone seldom rang during the day because everyone knew Jake and Ashley were working. Of course it could be Jude calling back with something new to report.

"Crenshaw residence," she said after picking up the phone.

"Uh, yes. I'd like to speak to Jason Crenshaw, please."

She froze at the sound of a voice she recognized. She'd heard it at the cabin when those men were looking for her. Leslie began to shake. How could they possibly have found her?

"Mr. Crenshaw is not here at the moment. May I have him call you?" She hoped her voice didn't betray her shock.

"When do you expect him? I'd really like to speak to him as soon as possible."

"I'm not sure. May I have your number?"

"I'll call back." The line went dead.

Had the deputies discovered that Jason was the one they'd met at the cabin? Did they know she had been there at the time?

She spun around and began to pace. After thinking about the situation for several minutes, she called Jake's cell phone.

"You bored yet?" Jake asked as he answered the phone.

"Uh, no. It seems that at least one of the deputies has tracked Jason down here. He called a little while ago wanting to talk to him. He said he'd call back."

"We'll be right there," he said, and hung up.

How could a mere phone call so completely rattle her? She knew she was safe on the ranch.

Plus, Jake and Jason would be here soon. She hoped. They'd taken the truck today, which meant they were farther away from the house than usual. Jason had a little trouble riding horseback for long periods of time.

Leslie paced. An amazingly short time later she heard the truck skid to a stop on the gravel near the house. She went into the kitchen to meet them. Jason was the first one through the door and when he saw Leslie he wasted no time getting to her. He pulled her against him so tightly she could scarcely breathe.

He held her until she stopped trembling before he leaned back and said, "They aren't going to harm you, honey. Didn't I promise? This may be the break we've been looking for in this case. I called Jude on our way to the house. He's contacting the FBI with this latest development."

She placed her head on his chest and felt his steady heartbeat. His warmth slowly seeped into her. When she finally lifted her head, she saw Jake leaning against the counter with his arms and ankles crossed, smiling with real amusement.

Leslie pulled away from Jason. "What's causing the smile?" she asked, feeling bewildered.

Jake grinned. "Oh, I find my brother rather amusing at times. I was driving as fast as the truck and road conditions allowed and Jason was yelling 'Hurry!' as though the world was collapsing and he had to get to you first."

Jason still held Leslie plastered against him. "I was wrong, okay? So don't rub it in any more than you have to. I didn't understand until she called and I knew those men had found her."

"Understand what?" she asked.

Jason glanced at her and kissed her on her nose. In a low voice, he said, "I'll talk to you later when we have more time. Meanwhile, here's the plan."

Four hours later the phone rang. Jake let it ring a couple of times before he answered.

"Crenshaw."

"Is this Jason Crenshaw?" a male voice asked.

"No. His brother."

"May I speak to him?"

"Sure."

He, Jason and Leslie had been waiting in Jake's office while Ashley had taken the children upstairs to bed. Jason waited a minute or so before he took the phone.

"Hello?"

"Jason Crenshaw?"

"You got him."

"I'm with the Deer Creek, Tennessee, sheriff's department. I understand that you recently married a Leslie Joanne O'Brien."

"That's right."

"Is she with you now?"

"Not at the moment."

"But she's living there with you?"

"I don't see where it's any of your business, but yes, that's what married couples seem to do."

There was a pause. "I'm curious to know how long you've known Ms. O'Brien."

"Mrs. Crenshaw," Jason corrected.

"Right. Mrs. Crenshaw."

"What difference does that make?"

"Are you aware she's an escaped felon and there's a warrant for her arrest?"

"What? What are you talking about?"

"She was convicted of murdering a city official in Deer Creek, Tennessee a few weeks ago. Somehow in the process of transferring her, she managed to escape. We've had a devil of a time finding her."

"You must be looking for someone else. Leslie's no killer."

"She fooled you, too, didn't she? She fooled a lot of

people. Evidence showed that while she worked in the office of the city auditor—by the way, you do know she's an accountant, don't you?"

"Yes."

"Anyway, she was caught embezzling county funds. At first we thought it was one of the city officials who'd turned up missing, until we found his body. It didn't take long to convict her."

Jason wondered if this guy had ever thought about writing screenplays with that kind of an imagination.

"I see."

"I know this is tough on you, but we need to arrange to pick her up. If you don't cooperate, we'll be forced to arrest you for obstruction of justice."

"Does the Deer Creek sheriff have jurisdiction in Texas?"

Another silence.

"Once we ascertain that we have the right person, we'll call the U.S. Marshal to formalize the proceedings. The thing is," the man went on with a more confidential tone, "she's been a real embarrassment for my partner and me since she was technically still in our jurisdiction when she escaped. We'd like to have her secured before notifying the proper authorities."

"This doesn't sound right to me. You must have her confused with someone else."

"We can certainly ascertain that once we see her."

Jason sighed. "I guess you're right. I sure don't want to be obstructing justice or breaking any laws."

"I understand you live in the country. Could you give us directions how to get there?"

"Sure." Jason gave him careful instructions and they hung up.

Jake, Jason and Leslie went across the hall to the den. "Did you get it?" Jake asked the four men sitting there.

Gus Emery, one of the FBI agents, nodded. "Yes, sir. I've got to believe that you wouldn't have called us in if he was telling the truth but I've got to admit he sounds convincing. I thought he'd trip up over the jurisdiction question, but he's quick on his feet."

Jason stood with his arm around Leslie's waist. "Their story has become more inventive since I first met them," he said. "But you're right. They come across as true blue deputies just doing their jobs."

Gus asked, "How long do you think it will take them to get here?"

"Depends where they're calling from."

Gus checked the tracer. "A motel in New Eden."

"Considering it's unfamiliar terrain and dark, I'd give them a good forty-five minutes," Jake said.

"Well, so far, so good. Here's hoping they'll incriminate themselves. Just don't spring the trap too soon."

Jason turned Leslie to him. "You still okay with this?" She nodded.

"I agree with the agents, I don't think they'll try anything until they get you alone and that's not going to happen. I'd like to get this nightmare over so we can get on with our lives."

"I know. You need to return to duty and I need to go back home to find a job."

"Uh, remember I told you that we'd discuss things when we had more time? I've got some suggestions I want to talk to you about regarding the future."

What did that mean? He hadn't let her out of his sight since he and Jake had arrived.

Whatever it was could wait. If she could get the two

to incriminate themselves, there would be no reason for her to testify at a trial.

She had enough incentive to give an Academy Award-worthy performance. She needed to remember that regardless of how it felt, she wasn't alone.

Fifteen

Jake strode through the foyer when he heard the knock at the front door. No one who knew the Crenshaws ever went to the front door, so there was no doubt in his mind who had arrived. He turned on the outside lights and opened the door.

Two men in uniform stood in front of him.

"Mr. Crenshaw?"

"Yes, I'm Jake Crenshaw. This is my home. Won't you come in?"

He watched the two men step inside and look around at the large foyer, its locally mined marble floor and the curving staircase that went to the second floor.

"Nice place you have," the younger, taller man said. Jase had told him the younger one was Leonard something or other.

"Thank you."

"I was to meet Jason and Leslie Crenshaw here," Leonard said when Jake said nothing more.

Jake nodded. "Come this way," he said, and led the way to his office. Once inside he said, "Have a seat, gentlemen. Unfortunately my brother was quite upset with your phone call, so he left without telling Leslie that you were coming. He said it would make things easier for you."

The deputies exchanged amused glances. "Smart fellow," Leonard said. "Where is *she?*"

"Oh, she's upstairs. Wait here and I'll get her for you."

Jake walked out of his office, closed the door and took the stairs two at time until he reached the hallway. Jason and Leslie stood in the shadows, his arm around her.

"So far, so good," Jake said. He gently squeezed Leslie's hand. "It's showtime."

Jason kissed her and murmured something in her ear that made her smile. "I'm ready," she said to Jake, and followed him down the stairs.

He opened the office door and said, "Here she is, gentlemen. Holler if you need anything."

As soon as Jake closed the door behind Leslie, Jason hurried down the stairs. The brothers went into the den and took seats.

Leslie froze when she saw the two men. "What are you two doing here?" She demanded. "And how did you find me?"

Bryce, the older one, said, "It wasn't easy, little lady. You've led us all around the country these past few weeks and wasted a great deal of our time."

Leonard motioned for her to take one of the chairs. "You know why we're here and you also know that your running is over."

Leslie ignored the chair Leonard had pointed out. Instead she went around the desk and sat in Jake's chair, putting the desk between them.

"I don't understand. I didn't see anything. Why won't you just leave me alone?"

Leonard stared at her in disgust. "You didn't see a thing, huh? Then how do you know who we are, huh? I know you saw me in the car chasing you down the street that night. Why didn't you stop when I blinked my lights…if you didn't see anything?"

"I promise I won't say a word to anyone. I haven't told a soul and I don't intend to. I'm married now. I'm starting a new life."

Bryce laughed. "Did you really think that changing your name would make a difference to us finding you? We're going to take you back to Tennessee. And just maybe, if you're extra nice to us, we might actually let you live until we get there."

Leonard scowled. "Shut up, Bryce."

"Why won't you leave me alone? I'm no threat to either one of you."

"That's not the way I see it," Leonard said with a cold smile. "The way I see it is, we came upon you right after you shot poor old Abner Wallace. When we jumped out of our car, you ran to yours and got away, despite everything we could do to catch you."

"I called the police as soon as I got home."

"That was mighty obliging of you. Saved us a lot of time, or so we thought. Only you didn't wait for us to show up."

"I got scared and ran."

"Uh-huh. Well, the game's over."

"There's no way you can make a murder charge stick and you know it. I don't own a gun. I never have. Much less a silencer. As soon as the judge hears the case—"

Bryce said, "Tell her, Leonard."

"It just so happens that the gun is registered in your name. We found it hidden in your car a day or so later."

"I never touched the gun. My prints were never on it."

"Yeah. You were real clever, wearing latex gloves."

"But you're making all of this up!" she said with a cry. Leslie didn't have to fake the trembling or the tears. She'd never been so close to evil incarnate before.

The office door opened. Leonard stood and said, "Thank you for the use of your office, Mr. Crenshaw—" and then he did a double take. "You!" he said to Jason. "You were up in the cabin in Michigan! She was right there with you all the time, you sneaking coward."

Jason stayed in the open doorway. "You two make good detectives, I've got to admit. I never thought you'd find her here."

Bryce shrugged. "The Internet is a good tool." He was now standing.

Leonard glanced at Bryce. "Looks like we're going to have to haul them both in. He's just as guilty as she is."

"That's absolutely true," Jason agreed. "Neither one of us is guilty of anything. I don't know who the hell you think you are, but you have no jurisdiction here in Texas."

Bryce looked at his partner. "Why, sure we—"

"Shut up," Leonard said. "We've spent too much time chasing this woman to let her go now."

Jason said, "At least be honest and tell me why you want her."

"I told you on the phone," Leonard said. "She was a witness to a crime."

Bryce nodded vigorously. "That's right."

"Funny, but that isn't what you told me on the phone. You said she was an escaped felon. Guess you'd better learn to keep your stories straight, being upstanding officers of the law and all."

"I saw them shoot another man," Leslie said, walking around the desk to stand beside Jason.

Bryce laughed. "You can't prove that. It's your word against ours. We found the gun in your car, with the fingerprints wiped off, of course."

Leslie leaned into Jason and said, "Don't let them take us. They're killers, Jason."

Jason patted her shoulders. "Why, honey, they're not going to take us anywhere because that would be kidnapping."

Leonard's pistol appeared in his hand. "Add it to our sins. Now, get moving. We're leaving now. If you try anything, I'm sure I'll be able to spot your brother somewhere around. Hell, I can take out the whole damn family if I want. It'll be an arrest gone wrong, that's all. We were forced to defend ourselves."

Jason looked at the pistol and into the eyes of a sociopath. The deputy wouldn't hesitate to the pull the trigger. This was the tricky part of the plan. When he and Jake discussed it with the FBI agents, they'd tried to factor in all eventualities, including that one of the deputies, or both of them, would pull a revolver.

"Well, Leslie," he said, sounding drained. "I guess we don't have much choice." He turned her and led her out into the hallway. Once out of sight, he pulled her behind him and waited.

Leonard and Bryce stepped out of the office and discovered they weren't the only law enforcement in the home. FBI agents surrounded them.

One of the agents said, "You're under arrest for the murder of Abner Wallace, attempted kidnapping and threatening a witness. Drop the gun and put your hands behind your backs."

The deputies looked at four pistols trained on them while the agent read them their rights. Leonard dropped the revolver on the floor and one of the agents kicked it out of the way and quickly cuffed them.

Jason whispered to Leslie. "I don't think they're going to need us. After what you've just gone through, you deserve to get away from these creeps."

Now that it was over, Leslie couldn't stop shaking. The adrenaline rush still surged through her body.

Jason kept his arm around her and they went upstairs.

Jason stopped at her bedroom door long enough to open it and they went inside. Leslie sat on the side of the bed and looked at him. "I can't believe it's over. This has been like some kind of nightmare and I couldn't wake up."

He sat at the end of the bed and leaned against the bedpost. "I hope you don't feel that the entire time has been a nightmare."

She turned to face him and put a pillow behind her. "Oh, Jason. Of course not. You saved my life. I'll be eternally grateful for all you—and your family—has done for me."

"Grateful."

"Till my dying day."

"Well, here's the thing. I've been giving our situation a lot of thought today, ever since we discovered you aren't pregnant. I finally faced the fact that I was disappointed."

She frowned. "That I was *not* pregnant?"

"I know. Surprised the hell out of me. I guess I'd been

so sure you were that my mind had raced ahead to make plans for the future."

"I'll admit I was a little sad, but we both know it's better this way. We can get on with our lives."

"I, uh, I was hoping that maybe we can get on with our lives together."

Leslie closed her eyes. This wasn't happening. This day had been much too full of surprises for her. "I need to go back to Deer Creek."

"I know."

"And you need to return to duty."

"I know."

"I don't want to be a military wife."

"I know."

She grew exasperated with him. "Then that takes care of any further discussion.

"Not necessarily. You need to go back to Deer Creek because you have an apartment there. You need to pack your things and move them out of there."

Her mouth fell open. "The FBI agents said that I would be safe enough in another few weeks to return to my life."

"What Jake was so amused about in the kitchen earlier was that I've been denying, over and over, that I'm in love with you."

Of course he wasn't.

"I finally admitted to him and to myself I was wrong. I'm crazy about you, Leslie Joanne O'Brien Crenshaw, and if there's one thing that I want more than anything it's to stay married to you."

"But, Jason—"

"Just hear me out, okay? Jake and I have been talking about my getting out of the service and moving back here. He knows of a ranch for sale. Actually, the land used to belong to the Crenshaws a hundred years ago and I'd like to reclaim it. I don't know how you'd feel about being a rancher's wife, but I figure it's better than being a military wife."

Leslie was the length of the bed away from him. She was dazed. Despite her feelings for him, perhaps because she loved him so, she'd been willing to let him go. Now she didn't have to.

"So what do you say? Will you marry me? Again? Jake was right. I cheated you and my family out of the celebration that goes with a big wedding."

"Jason, as much as I want to say yes, I'm too aware that neither of our lives has been normal since we met. I think we need to give this more thought. I know you've been restless, wanting to get back to your unit. I don't want to give you an answer until we're both sure this is the right thing. I never want you to regret changing your life around for me."

"You love me."

That was an easy one. "Of course I love you. I would have never made love to you if I didn't. I told you. I don't believe in casual affairs."

He frowned. "But we made love in Dallas! You knew back then that you loved me?"

"Absolutely. I refused to call it what it was. Instead, I worked to convince myself that it was an infatuation and that I'd get over it. That wasn't the case. I love you and I love living on the ranch. I just don't want you to regret your decision."

He moved closer and put his arms around her. "Oh, Leslie. You confound and confuse me until I don't know whether I'm up or down or sideways." He gently kissed her.

"I forgot to ask if you're feeling better."

"Some."

"Are we agreed that we'll stay married? I need to hear you say it."

She draped her arms around his neck. "Yes, Jason, we'll stay married. But let's don't plan a wedding just yet."

Sixteen

Leslie opened the door to her musty apartment and stepped inside. The plants were gone but nothing else had been disturbed. She turned and walked across the breezeway to Teri's apartment. After tapping on the door, she waited.

"Who is it?" she heard from the other side of the door.

"Teri, it's me. Leslie."

The door flew open as soon as she began to speak and Teri rushed out to greet her. "Omigosh, it is you. What a relief to see you again. C'mon in and we'll catch up on things."

Leslie looked over her shoulder at the door to her apartment. "Let me lock my door. I did a quick tour of my place and then I had to make sure that you were all right."

Once inside Teri's apartment, they helped themselves to coffee and settled into the living room.

"Have you seen the paper?" Teri asked. "The whole town's in an uproar. Actually the whole county."

"No. I just drove into town after two days on the road. Haven't seen a paper in days."

"You drove?"

Leslie nodded.

"You got a new car?" Teri asked with amazement.

"Half." She pointed down at the parking lot.

"Are you talking about that blue one? Surely not. So you borrowed it."

"Yes, I borrowed it from the other half owner. He had to report for duty."

"You and the soldier bought a car together. Right."

"Actually, we got married."

Teri stared at her in silence for a couple of minutes. "You're serious, aren't you?"

"Yes. We got married at the courthouse in Dallas. We're going to have the full-blown wedding with all its trimmings once Jason is released from the army. And I want you to be my matron of honor."

Teri, unflappable Teri, burst into tears. "You've only known him for—what?—a few weeks. This is so unlike you, Leslie. You've always been so sensible and so practical. What caused you to marry a man you don't know?"

Leslie smiled. "When you meet him, you'll know."

The day of Leslie's second wedding turned out to be cool and sunny, with a slight breeze. They declared it warm enough to have the wedding outside. Ashley had warned her that every Crenshaw would be at the ceremony, along with friends and neighbors. They all wanted to help Leslie and Jason celebrate. Joe planned to feed everyone once the wedding was over and Leslie expected to meet everyone who knew Jason, which seemed to be multitude or more.

Leslie hadn't seen Jason since he'd left several weeks ago, although they'd spoken daily on the phone. He'd arrived last night, according to Ashley, and she'd made him promise not to disturb Leslie the night before the ceremony. Ashley laughed when she told Leslie earlier today, saying she had to work at wringing a promise out of him.

Ashley, Lindsey—Jared's wife—and Gail were in Leslie's room putting the finishing touches to her hair, her dress, and her veil while Carina—Jude's wife—sat on the bed watching, her twins asleep nearby. Leslie had met Jason's other two brothers yesterday when they arrived. She and Jude had a deep discussion about the county where she'd lived and she had an opportunity to thank him in person for all he had done for her.

Leslie looked around at these Crenshaw women in wonder. She was one of them now, although Ashley was the only one who knew they were already married. Leslie had become part of this large, boisterous and solid family.

Teri stepped inside the door. "Okay, everything's ready for you. Are you nervous?"

Leslie shook her head. "Not in the least." She and Ashley exchanged a glance. "In fact, I'm eager to see Jase. It's been forever."

Teri said, "I can certainly see how you fell in love with your soldier."

"Former soldier."

Teri smiled. "All the Crenshaws have charm and charisma coming out of their fingertips." She looked around the room at the women. "It takes a strong woman to deal with them, I'm sure," and the women laughed.

When Leslie stepped into the hall, Joe Crenshaw was waiting. "I am so honored that you asked me to give you away."

"You're the only dad I've known. I couldn't have found a better one, anywhere."

"Be careful," Gail admonished as the rest of the women joined them on their way downstairs. "We can't let him get too puffed up or he'll be impossible to live with."

When Leslie stepped outside and saw Jason, everyone else faded away. He and Jake stood at the altar with the pastor, both wearing tuxedos that looked custom made, and both looking too handsome to be believed.

Teri walked down the aisle accompanied by the music and joined them. Leslie followed without taking her eyes off of Jason. As soon as he saw her, he grinned with such delight that tears formed in her eyes. She blinked quickly, not wanting to be crying when she reached his side.

As soon as she and Joe reached the others, Joe took her hand and placed it in Jason's, saying, "Take good care of her, son. She deserves all the love you can give her."

There was no holding back the tears. Jason used his thumb to gently wipe them away. "Welcome to my world, Mrs. Crenshaw," he murmured for her ears only. "This is where we begin to live happily ever after."

Epilogue

Jason walked down the hallway of the maternity ward still wearing his scrubs and paused in the doorway to the waiting room.

His mom and dad and his brothers with their wives looked up expectantly.

"Well?" Jake finally asked impatiently. "Is it here?"

"Yes. And just as we suspected, Leslie gave birth to a baby," he replied solemnly.

Gail laughed. "This is not the time to keep us all in suspense. Is Leslie all right? Is the baby healthy?"

He nodded. Jason tried to speak and had to clear his throat before he could talk around the lump that had lodged there. "Leslie and I have a daughter—Emily Ann Crenshaw. They're both worn out, though, and are resting."

"I should guess so!" Ashley replied. "She's been in

labor for more than twelve hours," she said, looking at her watch. "It's almost two o'clock in the morning."

Gail walked over and hugged him. "And how's the new daddy doing?" she whispered. He hugged her tightly and replied, "It was touch and go there for a while, I'll admit. I thought I was prepared for this after all those classes we took, but when I saw Leslie in so much pain and there was nothing I could do, I felt so damned helpless. I told her this was our first and last child."

His mother stepped back and looked at him. "And what was her response?"

He shook his head. "She was so exhausted she could hardly speak. She actually laughed at me. Go figure."

Joe spoke up. "Why don't we all go back to the ranch and get some sleep? We'll come see them in the morning."

His three brothers stretched and yawned, almost in unison. "Sounds like a plan," Jared said, dropping his arm around Lindsey. "I hate to think what your nanny is planning to do to us, Jake, for leaving all the young'uns with her for this long."

"Don't worry. She had them eating out of her hand when we left this afternoon."

Jason spoke to each one of them for a private moment before they left, promising to see him in the morning. Once they were gone, he went back to the room where Leslie waited.

The room was dim and he moved silently to the side of the bed. She lay with her eyes closed and still looked too pale as far as he was concerned. The doctor had assured him that she was just tired and would be fine by the next day.

He picked up her slim hand, which was resting on the

covers, and brought it to his lips. Her eyes opened slowly and she smiled. "We did it, didn't we?" she said softly.

"Honey, *you* did it. I was just there." He kissed her hand again. "I'm so proud of you."

"Isn't she gorgeous?"

He grinned. "I couldn't tell with that frown on her face. She wasn't at all pleased with any of us by the time she arrived."

"Yes. She definitely has her father's lousy disposition. But we'll work with her."

"That's not funny," he said, although he couldn't stop smiling.

"With her face all screwed up, I couldn't help but notice how much she looked like you when I first saw you."

"You're never going to let me forget that, are you?"

"Not a chance."

He sighed. "I'm better now."

"Oh? Let's ask Forrest, who has to work with you every day, shall we?"

"He's a good foreman and he tunes me out when he's had enough of my comments."

She watched him, her lids drooping. "Two cranky Crenshaws in my life. I hope I survive," she said, giving him a sleepy smile.

He leaned over and kissed her. "Well, this cranky Crenshaw is going home to bed. I'll be back later. Try to rest."

She nodded, closed her eyes and sighed with obvious contentment. Jason still had trouble believing his good luck at meeting this woman when they were both far away from their homes.

Some things were just meant to be, he supposed.

Later, as he got into his pickup, he thought, We have a whole new generation of Crenshaws arriving in an unsuspecting world. Hope the world's ready.

* * * * *

eHARLEQUIN.com

The Ultimate Destination for Women's Fiction

Visit eHarlequin.com's Bookstore today for today's most popular books at great prices.

- An extensive selection of romance books by top authors!

- Choose our convenient "bill me" option. No credit card required.

- New releases, Themed Collections and hard-to-find backlist.

- A sneak peek at upcoming books.

- Check out book excerpts, book summaries and Reader Recommendations from other members and post your own too.

- Find out what everybody's reading in Bestsellers.

- Save BIG with everyday discounts and exclusive online offers!

- Our Category Legend will help you select reading that's exactly right for you!

- Visit our Bargain Outlet often for huge savings and special offers!

- Sweepstakes offers. Enter for your chance to win special prizes, autographed books and more.

Your purchases are 100% guaranteed—so shop online at www.eHarlequin.com today!

Silhouette® Desire®

A violent storm.

A warm cabin.

One bed...for two strangers
stranded overnight.

Author

Bronwyn Jameson's

latest PRINCES OF THE OUTBACK novel
will sweep you off your feet and into
a world of privilege and passion!

Don't miss

The Ruthless Groom

Silhouette Desire #1691
Available November 2005

Only from Silhouette Books!

**Coming in November
from Silhouette Desire**

DYNASTIES: THE ASHTONS

*A family built on lies...brought together
by dark, passionate secrets*

continues with

SAVOR THE SEDUCTION

by Laura Wright

Grant Ashton came
to Napa Valley to discover the truth
about his family...but found so much
more. Was Anna Sheridan, a woman
battling her own demons, the answer
to all Grant's desires?

*Available this November wherever
Silhouette books are sold.*

COMING NEXT MONTH

#1687 SAVOR THE SEDUCTION—Laura Wright
Dynasties: The Ashtons
Scandals had rocked his family but only one woman was able to shake him to the core.

#1688 BOSS MAN—Diana Palmer
Long, Tall Texans
This tough-as-leather attorney never looked twice at his dedicated assistant…until now!

#1689 HIGHLY COMPROMISED POSITION—Sara Orwig
Texas Cattleman's Club: The Secret Diary
How could she have known the sexy stranger who fathered her child was her family's sworn enemy?

#1690 THE CHASE IS ON—Brenda Jackson
The Westmorelands
His lovely new neighbor was a sweet temptation this confirmed bachelor couldn't resist.

#1691 THE RUTHLESS GROOM—Bronwyn Jameson
Princes of the Outback
She delivered the news that his bride-to-be had run away…never expecting to be next on his "to wed" list.

#1692 MISTLETOE MANEUVERS—Margaret Alison
Mixing business with pleasure could only lead to a hostile takeover…and a whole lot of passion.

SDCNM1005